# THE YELLOW CAT CAFE

# THE YELLOW CAT CAFE

## CHINLE MILLER

~~Mangled~~ Modified excerpts from J.M.T. Miller's *Weatherby* are used with permission of the copyright holder.

Print ISBN: 978-1-948859-13-4

Cover by Cary Cox

*For my dear friend Steve*

*And for my sister Jan, who would have loved the irony.*

———

# CONTENTS

# 1

Sheriff Bud Shumway sat in the back booth of the Melon Rind Cafe, drinking coffee and absent-mindedly watching the traffic on the main drag of the little town of Green River, Utah. He needed to get to his office before long, but in the meantime, he was enjoying another typical slow start to his day.

The traffic hadn't taken much of his attention so far, as all he'd seen was three cars (one being the mayor on his way to work at his gas station), a couple of kids on bicycles, and Old Man Green on his antique tractor going who knows where, but probably to the library, as he'd developed a sudden interest in books after the new librarian had been hired.

Across from Bud sat his part-time deputy, Howie McPherson, who was reading the *New York Times*. Bud's wife, Wilma Jean, who owned the cafe, had a subscription to the paper, and Bud suspected it was so the townspeople would read it and thereby be appreciative of where they lived.

"Anything going on in the real world out there, Howie?" Bud asked.

"Well, here's an interesting article about a couple of kids whose parents are suing the high school of some town in Indiana because they won't give them their diplomas," Howie replied.

"That made the *New York Times*?" Bud asked, surprised.

"Yeah, well, it's kind of different," Howie replied. "It appears the kids are identical twins and took turns going to school. One would go one day, then the other would go the next day. The school's saying they're only half-educated."

Bud groaned, not sure if Howie was kidding or not. He now began fiddling with a fork, tapping a rhythm on the edge of the table, waiting for the waitress, Howie's wife Maureen, to refill his coffee cup.

Howie, now engrossed in another article, finally said, "I'll be darned, Sheriff! Maureen has this book. Maybe it'll be worth something someday."

"What book?"

"Well, some big New York publisher is pulling a best-selling book because the author apparently plagiarized part of it from her sister, a well-known mystery writer. The plagiarist claims the famous author gave her permission to use it, but the publisher's pulling the book anyway, and it's costing them a fortune. Do you think Maureen's copy will be worth something someday?"

"I don't know, Howie. I thought that kind of applied more to banned books, but who knows?" Bud replied.

"Maybe I should read it," Howie said. "Maureen always says I need to broaden my horizons. All I read is astronomy stuff, so maybe this would be a good one to start broadening with. I've actually never read a mystery."

"Me, neither," Bud replied. "From what I can gather, somebody usually gets killed or disappears. I have to deal with that kind of thing in real life, so I prefer reading about things like photography."

Howie said, "The book she plagiarized is called *On A Dead Man's Chest*, but her version's called *The Last Opera Show*."

"Was *On A Dead Man's Chest* a pirate mystery?" Bud asked.

"Probably lost treasure," Howie replied. "And if it's about treasure, maybe it has tips on how to use a metal detector. I need to get my Bounty Hunter Quick Draw back out and start messing around with it again. I did go around the park with it after Big Boy came to town, but I didn't find anything but some old nails from when they built the bandstand way back when."

"That steam engine was something else," Bud said, watching as Maureen seated a small dark-haired woman in a nearby booth. "But Howie, when is Maureen going to quit working? She's going to have that baby here in the cafe if she's not careful. Isn't that why Wilma Jean hired Karen's daughter, Heather, so Maureen could take some time off?"

Howie replied, "You know her, Sheriff, she's stubborn. She says she gets bored all day at home and wants to work as long as she can."

Howie now put the paper on the table, saying, "I need to get going. We're having the grand opening for Howie's Drive-In this weekend, and I need to go make some barbecue sauce."

"That's great, Howie. I'm glad you finally have everything ready, but you're going to be one busy guy, with a new baby and all, not to mention being a part-time deputy."

Maureen now handed the woman she'd just seated a menu, then came by Bud's booth and refilled their coffee cups.

Leaning over Bud and Howie, she whispered, "Don't look now, but that woman back there's a writer from New York."

"How do you know that?" Howie asked.

"See that little red sports car out there? That's hers, and it has New York plates. They're personalized and say IWRITE. And look at how she's dressed—all in black."

"Writers wear black?" Howie asked.

Maureen shook her head in irritation. "New York writers do. But I recognize her from the picture on the back cover of her new book, *The Last Opera Show*. Howie, run home and get it real fast so I can have her autograph it."

"You may not want to do that," Howie replied, showing Maureen the article in the paper.

Maureen put the coffee carafe on the table, sat down next to Howie, and began reading.

"What a shame," she said, putting the paper down. "It was a

pretty decent book. Maybe a bit too hard-boiled for my tastes in general, but the plot was interesting. It's about an opera singer who gets murdered, which I could totally understand."

Maureen stood and picked up the carafe, then whispered to Bud, "She asked me if a big guy had been around asking about Yellow Cat Flats. I told her I had no idea, but she could ask you, the local sheriff, so she may be coming back here. Be prepared."

"Yellow Cat Flats?" Bud asked in surprise. "Why in hellsbells would a writer from New York be interested in the Yellow Cat? That little car wouldn't make it past the first rut in the road. There's nothing out there but greasewood and rattlers."

"And old uranium mine adits," Howie added. "Maybe I should take my metal detector out there. I might find some cool stuff."

"Most of that cool stuff is now protected by the Federal Antiquities Act, Howie," Bud replied.

"Old U-Boom stuff?" Howie asked incredulously. "It's just junk."

"Well, the government now says the Uranium Boom Cold War stuff is historic and can't be removed," Bud replied. "Actually, I think it applies to anything over 50 years old."

"What's an adit?" Maureen asked.

"Basically just a hole in the ground," Howie replied, then added, "Old mine diggings."

Maureen answered, "Oh. Well, I need to go take her order."

But it was too late, for the woman had just left the cafe.

They watched as she got into the little red roadster and drove away, raising Bud's count of cars so far on Green River's main drag to four.

## 2

Bud waited patiently for Lindie to come back with the ball, but the little Carolina dingo seemed to have simply disappeared in a small dip in the hill. He called several times, then started walking in the direction he'd lobbed the ball, not intending for it to go so far.

He'd brought the dog out to the old Green River missile base to try to work with her, as he needed to make sure she wouldn't run off into the desert when he took her and his other two dogs for walks. He knew he was procrastinating going to the office, but nothing much ever happened around town anyway, and he did have his phone with him.

He'd left Hoppie, his Basset hound, and Pierre, his wiener dog, home while he took Lindie out, not wanting any distractions, for they were both good at ignoring him and chasing lizards and rabbits, though they never caught anything.

He didn't want their influence during this early stage of Lindie's training, as he knew she'd catch on to their bad little doggie ways soon enough. Neither Hoppie nor Pierre could run fast enough to elude Bud, but he knew Lindie easily could.

The old missile base from the Cold War days was perfect for dogs, and even though the buildings and towers were pretty much melting into the ground, this section where they'd once shot off the rockets had a tall chain-link fence around the perimeter that was still in good shape, keeping Lindie from going far. This made it a good place for dog-training, not that Bud considered his work with Lindie as such.

To him, it was more like dog conditioning, getting her used to his own lack of direction and discipline. He hadn't had her long, but he knew she was smart as a whip, and he hoped she'd learn to take pity on his lack of training skills and come back when he called her to get one of the dog treats in his pocket.

But so far his conditioning wasn't working, for call as he might, there was no sign of Lindie. He hurried down the road, once paved, but now a mishmash of chunks of asphalt and weeds, until he came to where he could see her only means of escape—the gate into the compound, where his old Toyota FJ was parked.

Sure enough, there sat Lindie, as if guarding his vehicle from a somewhat large fellow with a full beard who apparently belonged to a small white sedan parked nearby.

Bud again called Lindie, who, ignoring him, now lay down next to the FJ. Bud wasn't sure, but she seemed crouched, ready to jump up, a stance he recognized from when she'd once tried to jump a bear, though Bud had fortunately had her leashed. He was soon next to her, putting her in the FJ.

"That dog seems pretty serious," the man said. "Do you think she would've attacked me?"

"I don't think so," Bud replied. "I haven't had her long, but she seems to think she's a guard dog, so maybe if you had tried to get in my rig she would've. But I apologize if she scared you. There's usually nobody up here."

Bud now put a leash on Lindie and called her back out, introducing her to the man.

"This is Lindie," he said. "She's a Carolina dingo. The more people she meets, the better, so she can get more socialized."

Lindie now slowly wagged her tail as the man patted her head.

"A Carolina dingo? That's a new one on me," the man replied. "She does look like a nice dog. But I seem to be a bit lost. Can you point me to Yellow Cat Flats?"

Surprised, Bud glanced at the man's plates, noting they were from New York. Personalized, they read, "I-SING."

Bud wasn't one to pry, but he figured since the man seemed to be announcing it to the world, it was OK to ask.

"Are you a singer?"

The man, who seemed uncomfortable in what looked to be stiff brand-new jeans and a green plaid Western-style shirt, replied, "I am. I sing opera."

Bud wasn't sure what to say. He'd never met an opera singer before—in fact, he wasn't sure he'd ever even *heard* one. Finally, he replied, "That's your job?"

He immediately felt sheepish for saying it, but the man seemed unperturbed and answered, "Yes. I sing with the New York Met."

Bud, not sure if that was an orchestra or a museum, finally replied, "The New York Met? That's pretty prestigious, isn't it? I've heard it takes years to make your voice do that. What brings you to Yellow Cat Flats? Is there going to be some kind of artists' meeting out there or something?"

"Why would you ask that?" The man asked.

Bud suddenly felt wary and wished he hadn't said anything. Though he wasn't naturally suspicious, his job as sheriff included keeping an eye on things, and it seemed possible that this man had something to do with the writer in the cafe.

He replied, "Oh, I just can't picture an opera singer wanting to go out to the Yellow Cat. Not much there. But you need to get back on the freeway and go east. You'll see an exit in about 30 miles or so that reads *Yellowcat*—all one word—they didn't have room on the sign to make it two words, I guess. Go to your right, away from the Bookcliffs, and the road will eventually drop down off the Mancos formation into the Cedar Mountain and Morrison formations. That whole country's called the Yellow Cat, but like I said, there's not much out there. If it looks like rain, you'll want to get back out, as everything's expansive clays. But to be honest, I don't think I'd even try to take that car in there. Odds are good you'll get stuck. Most of the roads require high clearance, and some are even 4-by-4."

"Why do people go out there in the first place?" The opera singer asked.

Bud found it an odd question, but answered, "Normally about the only people out there are rockhounds or people interested in Cold War history, though you might meet an occasional paleontologist, as there's a couple of dinosaur quarries out there. Other than that, I have no idea."

"Well, I'll go see the country, I guess," the man replied. "But are there mountain lions?"

Bud nodded his head, "Probably, since I would guess that's where it got its name."

The man now said, "Back East we call them catamounts. My name's Jay Landowska. Thanks for the info."

Bud now wondered if Jay was afraid of getting eaten by lions and wanted to make sure someone knew who he was when they found him.

Jay then added, "I'm that baritone you hear when you listen to the Met's *Parsifal* or the *Barber of Seville*."

"I'm Sheriff Bud Shumway," Bud said, not telling Jay he'd never heard either opera—actually, he was pretty sure he'd never heard *any* opera, for that matter, as the local radio stations seemed stuck in country-western or classic rock modes.

When one got tired of listening to Sonny and Cher's *I Got You Babe*, sometimes you could pick up the Ute station over in Ignacio, Colorado and hear chanting and drumming—but for all Bud knew, they were chanting and drumming *I Got You Babe*. Since he didn't speak Ute, he couldn't tell.

Bud continued, "Be sure and stop by my wife's cafe, the Melon Rind, when you come through Green River, and good luck out there."

But Bud wasn't sure he'd heard him, for Jay was in his sedan, turning around on the old road and heading back toward town. Bud couldn't help but note that, like the writer in the cafe, the man had seemed to want to flee upon finding out an LEO was in the picture.

He shrugged his shoulders, put Lindie in the FJ, and headed back to his office, where he'd call his friend Sheriff Hum Stocks down in Radium, whose jurisdiction included Yellow Cat Flats, and ask if he knew about any strange goings-on out there.

# 3

Bud opened his office door to find Deputy Howie sitting at his desk, feet up. He appeared to be reading the book they'd talked about at the cafe.

Howie jumped as the door opened, putting his feet down, then relaxed when he saw it was Bud, putting his feet back up.

"I'm glad to see you feel comfortable here in your role of deputy," Bud said, grinning.

"Howdy, Sheriff," Howie replied. "I got used to this nice desk when I was sheriff—it's hard to break old habits. But I'm actually on my way to the drive-in. I had to run out and check on the cats, so I picked up Maureen's book. I stopped by to see if you wanted a barbecue sandwich later and then started reading while waiting for you. It's a bit of a page turner."

Howie held the book up, adding, "See, it's about this private eye who lives somewhere near the desert—I'm guessing southern California, though the author never says exactly where. His office is by the ocean, but he's currently out in the desert at some biker bar."

Bud studied the cover, which was set in lurid pinks and featured a somewhat portly woman wearing a horned Viking helmet who appeared to be singing her heart out while looking upwards at the title, *The Last Opera Show*.

In the lower portion of the cover was a montage of bad-looking motorcycle bikers, a werewolf, what appeared to be a private eye pointing a gun at someone, and a barnacle-encrusted treasure chest in the back of a pickup next to a body dressed in what Bud took to be a toga.

Howie said, "Listen to this," and started reading.

*The metallic thunder was growing louder. Motorcycles were screeching up to a halt, engines were being revved to maximum capacity, people were shouting orders and greetings over the din. Nails McNulty crashed through the front door. The bikers outside played with their accelerators, revving their engines, then letting them wind down, performing the evil orchestration that every bike club in the world uses as its formal announcement of arrival.*

Howie then added, "He's looking for the crooked county sheriff. And get this, the sheriff's name is Bryce—Bryce Canyon."

Bud grinned. "I'd probably feel cantankerous and crooked too, with a name like that."

"Nah, Sheriff, you'd just change it. You're not the type to go bad. But look here on the back cover."

*This engaging and gritty mystery introduces the world of P.I. Weatherby, who stands to become a favorite in the genre of hard-boiled detective mysteries. —The New York Times*

"Is this the same *New York Times* that printed the article about how the author plagiarized the book?" Bud asked.

"One and the same," Howie replied. "But what I'm wondering is why they don't get their reviews spell-checked."

"How so?" Bud asked.

"Well, P.I. should be P.E., Bud," Howie answered. "You know, for Private Eye."

Bud laughed. "Actually, Howie, it's for Private Investigator."

"Then why do they call them Private Eyes? Isn't it because they're hired privately to spy on things?"

"Well, you have a point there," Bud replied. "I'm actually not sure why. Maybe it's easier to write *Eye* than just *I*."

"It seems like it would be the opposite, since *I* only has one letter," Howie replied. "But maybe it's because *Private I* would look kind of weird in print. But they're both the same when you say them."

Now aware that he was somewhat willingly going down a rabbit hole, Bud quickly changed the subject.

"Say, any idea if that woman made it out to Yellow Cat Flats? She never got any directions from us, so I'm thinking she may have stopped at the Westwinds or something and asked there. But Howie, I just met a guy out at the missile base who was asking the same thing."

"That's odd," Howie said.

"I thought so, too," Bud replied.

"Obviously I'm not the only one confused by this P.I. versus P.E. thing," Howie said.

Bud groaned. "No, Howie, he was asking the same thing about how to get to Yellow Cat Flats, not why P.I. isn't P.E."

"OK, that makes more sense," Howie said. "Maybe there's some kind of convention going on out there. Or maybe they're testing some kind of new GPS."

"Well, I don't think either of them is going very far in the cars they're driving. That's rough country out there. Actually, I'm going to call Hum down in Radium and see if he's heard anything. Then I need to get Lindie home—she's out in my FJ and I don't trust her to not tear things up."

"Why not? Has she ever torn anything up?"

"Well, not to date, but she had a reputation for doing so when I got her."

"Just bring her into the office, Sheriff. She'll be a good dog if you'll let her."

"I think I'll do that," Bud replied, opening the office door. He was soon back, Lindie on a leash, wagging her tail, then sticking her wet nose in Howie's hand as a greeting, forcing him to pet her.

"I wish we had a dog," Howie said somewhat mournfully. "We were going to get one, but Maureen doesn't think it's a good idea with a new baby coming along. We decided to wait awhile."

"The cats and your little white bunny probably think that's a good idea," Bud replied. "But Howie, do you think this book you're reading has anything to do with a writer and an opera singer going out into the desert? Have you seen anything that might give you a clue?"

"There's an opera singer out there?" Howie asked in surprise.

"The guy who I met at the missile base said he sings opera."

"Oh, well, Sheriff, you have to give me all the facts if you want me to help you solve a mystery. The facts, just the facts."

"I've heard that somewhere before," Bud replied, though he wasn't sure Howie had really heard him, for his eyes were again glued to the book.

Finally, Howie said, "Listen to this, Bud. The P.E. left the bar and is out in the desert."

*It was one of those clear cold desert nights. The dark bleak highway stretched out before me. Once in a long while a pair of headlights would appear on the horizon. When the driver was close enough, he'd hit the dimmer and the headlights would beam down. And then the car or truck would grind toward and past me and I'd be alone again. A sliver of moon outlined the low bluffs and the haunted outcroppings of rock. The light etched out the ghostly forms of the saguaros and locoweed, the eerie grotesquely human outlines of the Joshua trees.*

"You can tell the detective's a city guy," Howie added. "I personally think Joshua trees are nice. I would never describe them that way. And outcroppings can't be haunted, it's impossible, since they're not sentient. And locoweed and Joshua trees and saguaros aren't even in the same ecosystem."

"Howie, most people don't know the difference. And if the P.I.

went around talking about how pretty things were, it wouldn't fit the hard-boiled genre," Bud replied.

"It kind of bothers me that people would see nature that way, Bud," Howie said. "That's all."

"Well, I doubt if most people do, Howie. You have to remember it's just a book. But I need to use the phone. I want to call Hum."

"Oh, sorry, Sheriff," Howie said, jumping up from the desk. "I need to get to work, anyway. I shouldn't have picked up this book."

"You can leave it here if you want," Bud offered.

Howie grinned. "Nah, then *you* wouldn't get anything done. I'll bring you a sandwich later this afternoon after I get the barbecue sauce finished. You can come to the drive-in tomorrow for another one at the grand opening, if you want."

"It's going to be a great day," Bud said. "It's been a long time coming."

"Yeah, I never should've sold it in the first place," Howie replied. "And when the guy quit paying, I shouldn't have waited so long to take it back. No offense to Wilma Jean, but we're going to have the best barbecue sandwiches in Utah."

"She would love that, Howie. She's all for having more businesses in town. She says it attracts more people when you have more amenities. Besides, her airplane catering service is keeping her plenty busy."

"That plane was a good idea, Bud. But I'll see you later."

With that, Howie was gone, leaving Bud craving barbecue, Lindie asleep at his feet.

# 4

Bud took out his phone, dialing a familiar number, especially since he'd once worked there.

"Radium County Sheriff's Office, Cal Murphy speaking."

"Cal, Bud Shumway. Anything going on down in your part of the country?" Bud asked.

"Oh, hello there, Bud. Nice hearing from you. Well, not all that much, just the usual tourists and all, now that spring's here. We did have a little wreck up on the mesa yesterday and had to fly a couple of mountain bikers out by chopper. And the river's running real high and the wetlands are starting to flood, so that could get interesting, especially since that hamburger honcho built his big fancy house smack in the middle of the flood plain, even though everyone warned him not to. But how are things up your way?"

Bud shook his head, glad he didn't have to deal with the chaos and mayhem Cal and Hum and their crew had to encounter every day during tourist season, as Radium was a popular place, being right next to a national park. Talking to Cal always made him feel appreciative of his little town of Green River in the middle of what Bud called the Big Empty.

"It's pretty quiet around here so far," Bud replied. "Howie's getting ready to reopen his drive-in, so you're all invited up for the grand opening this weekend—free barbecue. And I think you know Wilma Jean and I bought Krider's melon farm, so my hired guy, Kale, is getting the fields ready for planting. I'll be out there helping him pretty soon, but things are pretty slow right now."

Bud paused, then added, "But Cal, have you heard about anything going on out at Yellow Cat Flats? I've had a couple of folks from New York stop in and ask how to get out there, and it just seems a little odd."

Cal replied, "No, I haven't heard anything. They're probably just rockhounds. You know that Yellow Cat petrified redwood is quite the prize."

"Well, they sure didn't look like rockhounds, but maybe you're right, or they could be mineral dealers. Our annual rock and gem show just started. Would you mind keeping me advised if you hear of anything out there?"

"That's a big can do," Cal replied. "Actually, there is one thing sort of close to that area. The park's been getting repeated reports of theft out around the northern section, and they're wondering if it's not somebody coming in from that back road into the Yellow Cat."

"Theft?" Bud asked.

"Yeah, and it's mostly food type stuff, though one party reported someone taking their longjohns, of all things. They'd hung them on a juniper to dry."

"Are you sure it's not just ravens?"

Cal replied, "Well, it could be, but it seems to be going on about once a week or so, and ravens mess around all the time, they don't take breaks. They'll peck at things, but this is full-on stuff disappearing, like water jugs and things too heavy for birds. And the rangers have had to rescue people a couple of times who had all their gas siphoned. I know they're smart, but I've never heard of a raven that could do that."

Cal then added, "I think the park may have someone living out there. It would be pretty easy to hole up in that section without anyone knowing, especially when you get into that rough country over by the fins. Lots of deep little canyons and alcoves and such. But one of the park rangers thinks it's somebody living in the Yellow Cat. Apparently he's seen some tracks heading that way."

"Tracks?" Bud asked. "There have to be lots of tracks, given the number of people in the park. What exactly did he see?"

Cal replied, "He said it was tracks like some old narrow-tired vehicle, maybe like an old Willys Jeep. He said they were pretty distinct. He's seen them a number of times, especially after reports of theft. And you know, that reminds me of last summer when Hum and I responded to a call out in the Yellow Cat. I'd forgotten about this, but someone called in saying there were two old fellows stranded out there in the Poison Strip, over by the old Cactus Rat uranium mine. But hang on a second."

Bud waited patiently as Cal talked to someone in the background for a moment, then returned, adding, "Anyway, we went out and found them, but they weren't stranded. They told us they were prospecting, but it seemed kind of suspicious, as there were indications they were living out there. Maybe we need to take a little drive back out to see if they're still around. It would be illegal to squat on BLM land like that. The BLM rangers are too busy to get out there and check on things, since there's only two of them for this whole area."

Bud replied, "Well, if you do go out there, give me a call. I'd like to go along."

"Will do. But Bud, I gotta go, as someone's here to make a report about a stolen ATV. But on second thought, maybe we need to get on out there before things get even busier. Would this afternoon work for you?"

"You bet," Bud replied. "I'll have the cafe here pack us both a lunch."

"OK, sounds good. I'll meet you in front of the Silver Spur Cafe in Thompson at noon. That should give me time to finish up with this guy and get my things ready. Over."

Bud got a kick out of how Cal always said over instead of goodbye when on the phone, as if he were talking on a radio. Deputy

Cal Murphy was one of a kind, and Bud always enjoyed his company.

Bud was excited. He enjoyed going out with Cal, and for it to be work-related was even better. He'd call the cafe and have Maureen pack them lunches, tell Howie he'd be gone for the afternoon so he could cover for him, then let Wilma Jean know what was going on, though he was pretty sure she was gone, flying supplies in for a rafting party up at Sand Wash on the Green River.

He hadn't been out in the Yellow Cat for some time, and the thought of going back made him feel that old excitement he always felt when going out into the Big Empty.

But unbeknownst to him, he was about to see the wilds of his beloved desert in an entirely new way, as well as go on an adventure he would never forget.

# 5

Waiting for Maureen to call back, Bud pulled his harmonica from his shirt pocket and began trying to play a song Howie had written called "Guess Who's Back." It was about the Big Boy steam engine that had visited town not too long before.

It was a bit more complicated than he was used to, as he was still learning the instrument, but he thought he was capturing it pretty well when Maureen finally called to tell him the sack lunches were ready.

He would run by the cafe and pick them up, then go home and put the dogs in the yard with some Barkie Biscuits, leave Wilma Jean a note, then head out the 25 miles or so to the Silver Spur in Thompson Springs, where he would meet Cal.

As he got into his FJ, Bud flashed on what Maureen had said:

*It was a pretty decent book. Maybe a bit too hard-boiled for my tastes in general, but the plot was interesting. It's about an opera singer who supposedly gets murdered, which I could totally understand...*

It seemed odd to Bud that the author of that very book and an opera singer were now presumably somewhere out in Yellow Cat country. He wasn't sure if they were together or not, but something told him them being there at the same time was no coincidence.

He'd heard of a couple of cases where mystery writers had taken it upon themselves to use the very plots they'd conjured up to actually murder someone. Apparently, since they'd spent a lot of time researching murder methods for their books, they'd thereby decided to just go ahead and put all that research to use.

Was the writer from New York going to murder the opera singer? Would the last opera show for singer Jay Landowska be held out at Yellow Cat Flats?

Bud now wished he'd let Howie leave the book—it might have some valuable clues as to what was going on, including the method used to murder the opera singer. But why would a writer be so transparent? And why come all the way from New York to a remote Utah landscape to murder someone? Did she think the odds of the body being found were lower here than anywhere else?

Bud shrugged as he got out of the FJ and went into the Melon Rind Cafe to get the sack lunches. He knew that anyone willing to murder another human was rarely rational, but were instead usually at the mercy of their emotions.

After picking up the lunches, he then dropped Lindie off at the bungalow and was soon on his way. It wasn't long before he pulled up in front of the Silver Spur Cafe and parked next to a newer dark blue Ford club-cab pickup with the words "Radium County Sheriff" on its side.

Before Bud could get out of his FJ, Cal emerged from the cafe, carrying two cups of coffee. Handing Bud one, he said, "I was thinking we could ride together, but given those rough roads out there, we might be wise to go separate in case one of us gets stuck. Jackson said he got stuck out there just yesterday."

Bud knew that Jackson, the cafe owner, was a hard-core rockhound, spending much of his free time looking for agate and petrified wood he could polish and make into bolo ties, which he sold from a display stand in the cafe. He was a seasoned desert rat, and if *he* got stuck, things out there were pretty iffy.

"Sounds like a plan," Bud replied, handing Cal a sack lunch.

Cal said, "I need to get back before dark, as I have to feed the horses since my wife's out of town. Follow me."

Cal headed toward the freeway, Bud following, knowing that Cal was pretty fussy about his truck and didn't like to eat anyone's dust. Bud didn't mind, for in his opinion, the more dust on his FJ, the better it looked, as the dirt covered the desert pinstripes on its sides, scratches he'd gotten from bushes and whatnot.

They were soon at the Yellow Cat exit off the freeway where a sign read, *Exit 193, Yellowcat, No Services.* That same sign had read *Exit 190* for many years, Bud recalled, until the Utah Highway Department realized all the freeway signs were off by several miles and changed them, resulting in unknowing locals and freeway travelers alike complaining that mapmakers were no longer trustworthy.

They took a well-graded dirt road heading across the brown and yellow Mancos shales though low scrub, a road that Bud knew would drop off into the labyrinth of Yellow Cat country in about six or seven miles.

The road was deceptive, he thought, straight as an arrow, luring one into complacency before falling into a maw of confusion, a crisscross of old roads from the uranium boom days, many of which were now washed out and impassible.

They soon passed a sign that read: *Caution! Not the Road to Radium.* Bud smiled, knowing the story behind the sign and glad it was there.

He'd actually helped Hum put it up after a multi-day search for the wife of a Baptist pastor in Radium who'd mistaken the road for a shortcut on her way back from Colorado.

She'd gotten stuck and been lost for several days, wandering and singing hymns, eventually making her way down Lost Spring Canyon to Salt Wash on the northern side of the park. There she'd finally been found by search-and-rescue a mere day before a major blizzard shut the entire region down.

Continuing on, Bud and Cal passed an old corral with a cattle loading chute. Shortly thereafter, Bud saw something he'd never seen out there before—a mailbox by the side of the road.

Cal had already stopped, and Bud pulled over, puzzled, though he suspected it had been put there by rockhounds who visited the area as a way to pass messages to one another.

"This is new," Cal said, as he and Bud both got out.

"Looks like it was borrowed from the Desert Star Hotel in Thompson," Bud commented, pointing to where someone had tried to scuff out the name on the mailbox. Presumably, that same someone had used a black marker to write across the front of the mailbox: *No junk.* Written in large letters on the side were the words: *If flag up, take to post office 4 free coffee. Yellow Cat Cafe*

The flag was down, but Bud looked inside anyway.

"Nope, no letter," he said, pulling out a small brown piece of rock. "Though it does look like someone put a piece of petrified wood inside. Does the post office give you a free cup of coffee, or does the cafe—assuming you can find it?" Bud grinned, then added, "Could this have something to do with the two guys you mentioned were maybe living out here, Cal?"

Cal shook his head in frustration. "It looks like they've established residency, for sure, Bud," he said. "Especially if they have a cafe, which seems pretty unlikely, unless they just serve themselves. You think if we put an eviction notice in there they'd get it?"

Bud replied, "It says no junk, Cal. I have a feeling that anything not edible or spendable is junk to them."

"I guess we'll have to serve notice in person then," Cal said. "They seem kind of cocky about their right to be out here, putting up a mailbox—and starting a supposed cafe."

"Well, it *is* public lands," Bud half-kidded. "Seems if I understand the BLM rules, they can squat for 14 days before having to move."

"Well, the Bureau of Land Management prefers people to camp, not to squat," Cal replied. "And Hum and I came out here at least six months ago, so I'd say they're a bit over their limit, and a cafe would definitely be illegal. But let's head on out and see what we can find."

They were soon winding down through cliffbands of buff-colored

Cedar Mountain formation, famous for deposits of dinosaur bones. The road grader had obviously stopped at the top and gone home, for the road was now rough and rutted.

Now at the bottom of the cliffs, the road split, and Cal took the branch that went east. Bud knew this was the way to what was called the Poison Strip, where the majority of the old uranium mines had been.

The name came from the fact that the soils were high in selenium and other toxic minerals, a fact underscored by the lack of vegetation, as well as the fact that if one were thirsty and lucky enough to find standing water anywhere, it was likely to make you sick, if not worse.

Bud recalled an old book from the U-Boom days of the 1950s he'd seen in the Green River Library titled: *Uranium Indicator Plants, Botanical Prospecting for Uranium Deposits.* It had been put out by the AEC, or Atomic Energy Commission, to help uranium prospectors, and listed the plants, like prince's plume and vetch, or locoweed, that grew in selenium- and sulphur-rich soils, minerals associated with uranium. Many of these plants were also poisonous.

It could be a harsh place to make a living, whether you were plant or animal, Bud mused. In addition to the toxic minerals, the desert got cold in the winter and hot in the summer, and other than the first stretch of six miles or so, which gave basic access to the area, the roads weren't maintained by the county.

Yellow Cat country kind of epitomized the solitude and emptiness that Bud loved, except for the junk left from the mining days, and even that could be interesting and photogenic, like the old rusty truck they'd just passed, slowly sinking into the ground, its windows shattered by bullet holes.

But even more interesting to Bud was the little white sedan ahead that appeared to be sunk into the deep ruts in the road, a sedan that had New York plates that read I-SING and which appeared to be abandoned.

## 6

Bud and Cal both walked around the car, examining its state of burial. Checking the doors, Cal found the driver's side unlocked, and on the front seat were a couple of hamburger wrappers and a hard-bound book, which Cal handed to Bud.

Bud said, "Cal, this is the same book Howie's wife has a copy of. It's by the writer who was asking about how to get out here, and this car belongs to the opera singer I told you about."

Bud opened the book, where he noticed an inscription in a precise, fine handwriting: *For Jay. Love, Marie.*

Bud looked at the front of the book—the author was Marie Lee. If the inscription was by the same Marie as the writer, it confirmed that she and Jay did indeed know each other, and pretty well. Bud put the book back on the front seat.

"We need to get this car unstuck," Cal was saying. "So the road's passable. It's blocking everything. Do you suppose the fellow got a ride out?"

Cal was now rummaging around the back seat of the car.

"Bud, lookie here. A pair of jeans and a shirt, all neatly folded. They look brand new. Do you recall what the opera guy was wearing?"

"These are definitely his clothes," Bud replied. "But why would he take them off, neatly fold them, then leave?"

Cal said, "Hey, we're in luck! Here's his keys in his pants pocket." He then added, "So, we have an opera singer out here in the Yellow Cat running around hopefully in at least his BVDs—that's kind of a thought. But we need to find this guy pretty soon, Bud, or we may be doing a body recovery, as it's too chilly to be running around half naked."

"Agreed," Bud said. "I predicted he was going to get himself into trouble when he told me he was coming out here, but I sure didn't expect it to happen so quickly."

Cal replied, "I have a tow strap in my truck. Let's pull this off to the side of the road, then we can see if we can find this guy."

They quickly had the vehicle unstuck, leaving it by the road, the keys back in the man's pants pocket in case he should return.

"That made me hungry," Cal said, pulling out his sack lunch. "What's in this, anyway?"

"A couple of roast-beef sandwiches, some chips, and a piece of chocolate cake," Bud replied. "But I'm going to look around a little more, Cal."

Bud started scanning the area and soon found a set of tracks where someone had walked through the mud. The tracks were going down the road in what Bud considered to be the wrong direction—instead of walking out, they were going farther into the Yellow Cat.

"Hey, Cal," Bud yelled. "Tracks. Follow me in your truck when you're done eating."

"That's a big can do," Cal replied, holding up a sandwich.

Bud continued following the tracks, which disappeared after about a quarter mile or so. He walked on, but could find no sign of anything.

He now began backtracking—had he missed something? Finally, scanning both sides of the road carefully, he found where the tracks had veered off onto a large flat outcropping of sandstone, which he knew would be impossible to track anyone across.

Cal had now caught up to Bud. "Any sign of him?" He asked, leaning out his pickup window.

"I lost him," Bud replied.

"He may be up in the rocks over there," Cal said, pointing at an outcropping a few hundred feet above them.

As Bud looked over to where Cal pointed, he heard something completely new. Like the mailbox in the desert, it was something he'd never experienced before, in spite of all his years of exploration in the backcountry.

Someone with a rich baritone voice was singing, and it sounded like it was coming from the rocks above, echoing from the cliffs around them.

*Figaro, Figaro, Fiiii-garrrr-ohh!*

Now he could make out a large man in the distance standing on a rock, arms extended in a dramatic pose.

"He's disoriented," Bud said. "Maybe hypothermic. He thinks he's at the opera. Let's go, Cal."

Cal jumped out of his pickup, and he and Bud made their way toward the man, huffing and puffing up the steep slope, but when they got there, he was nowhere to be seen. They sat on a rock, catching their breath, puzzled at where the man could have gone.

Suddenly, the guy stepped out from behind the rocks, wearing hiking boots, sweat pants, a sweater, and carrying a small pack.

Now the man said, "Singing opera, like getting drunk, is a sin that carries its own punishment. You guys looking for someone?"

With that, Jay Landowska sat down on the rocks next to Bud and Cal, offering them sticks of red licorice from his pack.

To Bud, it seemed like Jay acted more like he'd just joined them for a picnic in Central Park as opposed to being lost in the Yellow Cat, one of the most remote and harsh landscapes in the continental United States.

Not knowing what to say, he and Cal both just sat there, catching their breath.

## 7

---

Bud, Cal, and Jay all sat on the rocks, eating licorice while surveying the wide vistas of Yellow Cat country.

"So," Cal asked Jay, "You're saying you got stuck, changed into more comfortable clothes, then started walking down the road, hoping for a ride, out here in one of the least visited places in the Lower 48?"

"Yes, and I finally climbed up in the rocks here to get a good look at everything, to see if I could maybe spot the cafe," Jay replied.

"Did you know that there was a cafe out here from seeing the mailbox?" Bud asked.

"Mailbox? No, I met two fellows who asked where I was going, and they told me about the cafe."

"And they didn't help you get unstuck?" Cal asked.

"I wasn't stuck then. They stopped my car and asked what I was doing out here."

"They actually stopped your car?" Cal asked in disbelief.

Jay looked puzzled. "Isn't that what people normally do out here? They told me they were just checking on things."

"Were they BLM rangers or something?" Bud asked.

"No, they were in an old army ambulance. There were two of

them. Both looked somewhat—well, I guess the word would be grizzled."

"More like unwashed and grizzled, if it's who I think it is," Cal replied. "And for the record, no, people don't usually stop each other out here and ask what they're doing."

"What about sheriff's deputies and such?" Jay asked, nodding at the insignias on Bud and Cal's shirts.

"Usually no," Bud replied. "Not unless there's a good reason for it."

"More licorice?" Jay asked, digging into his pack.

"No thanks," Cal said. "But do you have any food and water in there?"

"A little of both," Jay replied. "Licorice, a water bottle, and some road cookies. Are you hungry?"

"And you were going to just wander around out here until you came to some supposed cafe? Didn't that strike you as a bit iffy?" Cal asked.

"Well, normally, yes," Jay responded a bit testily. "And now I'm beginning to feel like you're doing the exact same thing you said wasn't proper etiquette out here, asking me my business."

"Jay, our business sometimes involves retrieving bodies, and we're just making sure that a dead body doesn't also become *your* business," Bud said.

Now Jay looked perturbed. "Bodies? Dead people? Why would I have anything to do with dead people? Or are you talking about *my* dead body?"

Bud badly wanted to ask Jay what he was doing out here, but he didn't expect to get a different answer from when he'd asked earlier and Jay had said he just wanted to see the country.

Now Bud asked, "What exactly are road cookies?"

Jay, looking relieved at the change of subject, replied, "Oh, they're just any kind of cookie that's easy to eat while driving. I usually like Fig Newtons—not crumbly and all that. You don't mess up your car."

Bud thought of the mud splattered all over Jay's car where it now sat back along the road.

Cal asked, "So, do you have any idea where this so-called cafe actually is?"

"I do, officer," Jay said, now apparently aware he was going to be interrogated regardless of what was considered proper etiquette. "The two fellows said it was a few miles up the road here. I figured I could go find them and they'd help me get unstuck."

"What were their names?" Cal asked.

"I didn't get them," Jay said. "They just said the cafe was called the Yellow Cat Cafe, and I should stop and have a cup of coffee when in the area. One was quite congenial, though the other was a bit crusty. He seemed a little miffed that I'd come out here without bringing them something to eat. How could I bring them something to eat when I didn't even know they were here? Besides, if they run a cafe they should have plenty to eat."

"They're not supposed to be living out here," Cal said with disgust. "These are public lands. And now it sounds like they're stopping people like they own the place."

"You mean this belongs to everyone?" Jay looked skeptical.

"Yes," Cal replied. "Public means United States citizens. It's managed for us by various federal agencies, in this case, the Bureau of Land Management. By the way, we got your car unstuck, and since you left the keys in your pants pocket, maybe we should get back and retrieve it."

Jay looked horrified. "I left my keys? Oh no! I can't afford to have it stolen. I've never left my keys like that."

"Maybe you're cold and disoriented," Cal said. "That's the kind of thing people do when their mind gets cloudy."

"I'm not a bit cold," Jay replied. "Or cloudy."

"You were singing up here in the rocks," Cal said as if to make his point.

"I sing," Jay said somewhat petulantly, as if Cal should know that.

"You could probably leave your car with the keys in the ignition and it would still be there a year from now," Bud replied. "This isn't New York. Nobody comes out here, and the ones who do wouldn't be very likely to steal a car."

"I guess you were right about me not bringing it out here," Jay said. "But where's your dog?"

"She's home," Bud replied as they all stood and started back down the hill, Cal leading.

"Speaking of dead bodies," Jay said, walking behind Bud, "What happens when people get lost out here? Does it happen very often?"

"Not so much out here," Bud replied. "Not very many people come into the Yellow Cat, and those who do are usually prepared, people like rockhounds or geologists. But when people do get lost, the authorities call out search-and-rescue. Cal deals with lost people all the time where he's at, as the area attracts lots of folks who know nothing about the wilds. Maybe like your writer friend? Is she out here?"

Bud thought back to the inscription in the book from Marie Lee to Jay, as well as the person in the cafe, who he presumed to be Marie. He'd been hesitant to ask, but the question had just popped out.

Jay was silent for a long time, then finally said, "I don't know where she is. Last time I saw her, she was in New York. That was some time ago."

Bud now stopped and turned around, facing Jay, who also stopped.

"The woman who wrote that book was in the cafe in Green River just this morning," Bud said. "I can't imagine why she would want to come out here. Do you have any idea?"

Jay looked at the ground, then said, "I have no idea. But maybe we're talking about two different people."

Bud asked, "Didn't she write that book that you have in your car?"

Jay sighed, and being a big guy, the sigh was deep and long. Finally, he said, "That would be Marie. She got in some trouble with that publisher and is maybe looking to get away from all the publicity for awhile, is my guess. She actually never told me that, it's just what I think may be going on. We just got divorced. She doesn't tell me where she's going any more."

"You're not out here looking for her? Not just wanting to see the country?" Bud asked.

Cal had now stopped and was waiting, seeing that Bud and Jay were far behind.

Jay, saying nothing, resumed walking.

As he passed Bud, he said, "I saw a show once on search-and-rescue dogs. Your dog would be good at that. Maybe I could borrow her for awhile."

Bud was taken aback, not sure what to say, wondering why Jay would want to borrow her, and the three of them were soon back at Cal's truck.

Once back at his car, Jay thanked them for their help, then, taking Cal's advice, headed back toward civilization. The sun was beginning to set, and Bud and Cal tarried awhile, finishing their sack lunches.

"I need to get home and feed," Cal replied.

"I left the dogs in the yard," Bud said. "They're going to think they've been abandoned." He wondered if Lindie was being good or if she'd found some bad and creative way to entertain herself.

Just then, a bright yellow Jeep Cherokee drove up and stopped. It had large knobby tires, a winch on the front, a large hitch on the back, and the words *Tanner Towing and Off-Road Recovery* on the side, along with various dents and scratches.

"Afternoon," a congenial-looking man said, leaning out the window. "You fellows seen anyone stuck? Oh, hi, Cal. Nice seeing you."

"There was a guy stuck up the road, but we got him out," Cal replied.

The man, looking disappointed, said, "Guess I drove all the way from Radium for nothing. You guys are cutting into my business."

He frowned, then quickly turned around and drove away, leaving Bud and Cal both puzzled. Jay hadn't mentioned calling a tow truck, and if he had, why hadn't he waited instead of trying to find the cafe?

"He sure seemed in a hurry to get out of here," Cal said.

"Maybe it has something to do with us being LEOs," Bud replied. "It wouldn't be the first time."

"That's Tex Tanner. He lives in Radium," Cal replied. "Somebody must've been out here and called in Jay's car, which seems odd, as usually one would call the sheriff about an abandoned vehicle, not a tow truck." Cal now got into his pickup. "We're going to have to try this again later, Bud. I'll be in touch."

Bud followed in his FJ back up the hill through the cliffs, past the mailbox and old corral and finally to the freeway, where he stopped and tried to call Wilma Jean. It went to her voice mail, so he figured she was probably still in the air.

He'd go back to Green River, stopping by Howie's Drive-In for that barbecue sandwich, then go on home. Shading his eyes from the setting sun, he wondered where Jay was going next. He thought back to what Jay had said about wanting to borrow Lindie.

Whatever he'd meant by it, Bud suspected it had something to do with Marie Lee, wherever she was, and *The Last Opera Show*.

# 8

---

Bud sat at a picnic table in front of Howie's Drive-In, eating the second best barbecue-beef sandwich he'd ever had, the first best having been the previous evening when he'd stopped by to see how things were going on his way back from the Yellow Cat.

He wondered how Howie had managed to so expertly mix a perfect hint of sweet with a touch of tomato bite. He'd have to ask him his secret later, when he wasn't so busy.

The line for free sandwiches went halfway down the block, and Bud recognized people he hadn't seen in some time, as well as some he saw every day—Old Man Green, Junkyard Goldie, Frosty and Eldon of the Bucket of Bolts Overlanders, Sammy from the airport, Karen from the Chow-Down, fellow watermelon grower Larry Digham, and even some employees from the state park. Wilma Jean had already come and gone, now helping Maureen at the Melon Rind, though Bud suspected they didn't have much business.

Everyone seemed to be having a great time, and Bud could see Howie through the big window serving sandwiches, Karen's daughter Heather giving him a hand. He looked stressed and yet happy, and Bud knew then and there that the drive-in would be a big success.

He wondered if it might even eventually lead to Howie resigning from being his part-time deputy, though he hoped not. But having a baby would certainly add to that probability, for he didn't see how Howie could keep up with everything.

Just then, Bud's phone rang, and he could see from the caller-ID it was the Radium County Sheriff's Office. He wondered if Cal might be calling to see if he wanted to go back out to the Yellow Cat, since they hadn't spent that much time out there looking around the previous day.

"Yell-ow," Bud answered, wiping barbecue sauce from his hands.

"Bud, this is Cal. Is this a good time to talk?"

"Sure," Bud replied, noting Cal sounded serious. "What's going on?"

"Hum and I just got back from Yellow Cat Flats—a body recovery. Bud, it was a woman, maybe in her forties, and it looked to us she'd been out there for a day or so."

Bud asked, "Did it look like foul play? Where did you find her?"

Cal continued. "She was down by the old Ringtail Mine, a hundred yards or so from her car. How she even got it back in there is beyond me, a little red roadster. She called 911, saying she was sick. None of us could find anything indicating any foul play, heck, we couldn't find anything even indicating how she died, though she said she'd been poisoned. It was like she went to sleep next to a rock. We'll know more after the autopsy, but it sure seemed strange, especially given what you told me about people from New York going out there. And the timing seemed strange, too, Bud, since she made the call today, but the coroner said he thought the body was out there at least since yesterday, though he won't know for sure until he does his autopsy."

Bud suddenly felt a strange foreboding, like this might have something to do with the woman who'd come into the Melon Rind the previous day.

He asked, "Cal, did the red roadster have New York plates, and was she dressed in black, kind of a small gal?"

"You got it, Bud. Was this one of the people you mentioned?"

"It sounds just like the woman who came into the cafe yesterday asking how to get to the Yellow Cat."

Bud now thought of Jay, wondering where he was. He asked, "Did you see anyone else out there, like maybe that opera guy?"

"Nope, not a soul. Bud, Tex Tanner's recovering her car, but I thought maybe you could go check things out and see if you can come up with anything. We need some ideas. It's sure puzzling. The coroner was pretty sure she'd been dead at least a day, so I don't see how she could've been in the cafe. Yet the call came in today, so maybe the coroner's wrong, but he's a pretty knowledgeable guy. But would you have time to go out there?"

Bud thought for a moment, then answered, "My normally swamped schedule is empty today, Cal. I can head out there ASAP. Do you have the GPS coordinates?"

"I do. You have something to write them on?"

"Actually, no, but call me back and leave them on my voice mail. I'm at Howie's grand opening having a sandwich. I'll run home and get a few things, then head on out. Was there anything else you found of interest?"

"Nothing except a small notebook she was carrying. It had a sketch of a plant in it, but nothing else."

"Can you fax a copy of it to my office?"

"That's a big can do," Cal replied.

Bud said, "I'll give you a call if I find anything, assuming there's cell service."

Cal replied, "I'll call you when we know more. Anyway, thanks for your help. Over."

"Not a problem," Bud replied, hanging up.

He nodded as Mrs. Jensen from the Palatial Estates Trailer Park walked by, noting how she was dressed in her Sunday finest and looked much less stoved up than usual. She fluffed her hair out a bit as she approached Frosty Merriott, who was waiting in the sandwich line. Bud noted she'd dyed her normally gray hair a platinum blonde.

Frosty tried to duck away, but she soon had his arm in a vise grip, smiling and saying something about how nice he looked. Eldon watched, not even trying to hide his delight as Frosty looked chagrined.

Bud wondered if she might join the BOB-O's, Eldon and Frosty's Bucket of Bolts Overlanders, whose expeditions were strict about using clothing and equipment from the good old days. He could easily see her wearing a pantsuit or dress from the 50s or 60s, but for some reason, he couldn't really see her out in the backcountry bouncing around in Frosty's old Jeep, though he knew stranger things had happened.

Bud stood, greeted several others in line, then got into his FJ. He'd stop by his office and get the fax, then go get the dogs, as he knew they'd enjoy a ride out into the desert.

Maybe he could even find a little time to take some photos, as it was another beautiful spring day out in the Big Empty, one of his favorite times of the year, when many of the desert wildflowers were in bloom, though knowing the woman had died threw a pallor over things.

He was curious as to where Jay Landowska was and if he knew about his ex-wife's death, or had even somehow been involved.

Bud thought back to how he'd wondered if somehow the writer from New York was going to murder Jay, and how the last opera show would be held out at Yellow Cat Flats. Had she tried and somehow been foiled by Jay, then he'd instead killed her? Maybe he was out in the Yellow Cat right now, serenading the rocks in operatic triumph.

Bud shook his head at the thought, for Jay really hadn't seemed like that kind of guy—he seemed more like a bumbler than a murderer. And if the coroner was right about when she'd died, then things got more complicated, Bud thought. If she'd died the previous day, who'd made the 911 call today?

He headed for his office, not sure what he could do to help Hum and Cal, but he knew he'd sure try, and he was happy to be able to give it his best shot.

# 9

---

Bud sat at his desk, studying the page Cal had faxed, wondering if it had any significance or was related to the woman's death in any way.

It was a well-done sketch of a somewhat small but airy-looking plant with flowers that held what looked to be bell-shaped pods. Written under the plant in a delicate but no-nonsense script was the description:

> Preuss poisonvetch
>
> Purple irregular flowers. Blooms in April and May. Perennial. Has many stems less than a foot high arising from a woody base. Garlic-like odor of foliage is due to presence of selenium. Highly toxic.
>
> Common on mine dumps and along outcrops of ore-bearing beds where selenium and vanadium are available. Mineralized ground exists under these plants in Yellow Cat Flats, Utah, where a subspecies with a beautiful yellow calyx may be endemic.

The words, *Yellow Cat, yellow calyx,* and *endemic* were all underlined, and in the margin were the words, *What color!*

Bud was mystified and wondered if he could be looking at something important. Just then, his phone rang, and seeing it was Cal, he didn't answer, but instead let it go to voice mail. He then retrieved the message, writing the GPS coordinates on the faxed page.

He was soon on his way out to Yellow Cat Flats in his FJ, Lindie at his side in the passenger seat, and Hoppie and Pierre in the back. He had a thermos of coffee, some sandwiches, and a big slice of Wilma Jean's homemade apple pie, as well as plenty of water and biscuits for the dogs, and his camera. Even though Howie was busy at the drive-in and unable to cover for him, Bud didn't expect to be gone all that long and had left the office phone forwarded to the state patrol office.

He took the freeway exit, passed a couple of fellows unloading dirt bikes, then headed on down the straight-shot road, a rooster-tail of dust following close behind. He could also see dust settling just ahead of him and knew someone had recently come this way, probably rockhounds, since it was the weekend.

He'd almost gone past the mailbox when he noticed the flag was up. He quickly pulled off the road, let the dogs out for a minute, then opened the box and looked inside. Sure enough, there was a letter, and as he took it out, he was surprised to see it was addressed to the Sheriff of Emery County.

The envelope was old and yellowed, with the previous address marked out, though Bud could still make out *Union Carbide Nuclear Co., Mining Division, Dove Creek, Colo. Attn. Arthur Marinelli.*

The envelope bore three four-cent stamps with Abraham Lincoln's picture and a cancelled date of July 2, 1961. The return address had once read *Cordray Electric, P.O. Box 1061, Radium, Utah*, but was now also marked out and replaced with *YC Cafe.*

Bud wondered why anyone would send him a letter from out in the Yellow Cat when it wasn't even in his county or jurisdiction.

He slowly opened it and read:

*Dear Sheriff,*

*I know you're not the sheriff in these parts, but I'm hopin' you can help us out anyway, since Sheriff Stocks over in Radium's pretty busy these days. Something strange is goin' on out here. A woman all dressed in black stopped by, askin' directions. She was drivin' a little red sports car with*

*New York plates. Not too long after, we were out scouting around for* ~~tourists~~ *rocks when we ran into another car from New York, and this one had a big bearded guy in it. We stopped him to find out what he was doing, being good neighborhood-watch citizens and all, and he asked if we'd seen the woman. I started to tell him we had, but my buddy Leon stomped my foot.*

*I'm thinkin' that maybe they're either claim jumpers or some kind of developers. Either way, you might wanna come on out here and take care of things, since that's your job as sheriff.*

*If you do come out, be sure to stop by the Yeller Cat Cafe and we'll give you a cup of mud as long as you bring some with you. We like that kind called Wicked Brew. It's roasted by some of them folks up in Salt Lake. Bring some of them little goldfish crackers when you come, and some Redhead Matches. A few sticks of dynomite would be good, too.*

*Yer pal, Jasper*

*P.S. We've been hearin' somethin' strange out in the distance. You might wanna tell the Holyoaks one of their bulls is lost out here.*

*P.P.S. I dictated this to my buddy Leon, and I hope he stuck to what I told him. (Leon here - I always have to do all the writing, 'cause Jasper's illiterate, and yes, I did stick to what he said, though I made him sound smarter than he really is.)*

Bud shook his head in disbelief. This had to be the pair Cal had told him about, but for them to actually be writing to him seemed a bit far-fetched. And the handwriting seemed out of place—full of flourishes like something from a past century.

He now noticed that Pierre had discovered a prairie-dog hole and was starting to dig, his eyes taking on that glazed look that dachshunds get when focused on going after something. Since Bud could now hear the dirt bikers coming in the distance, he gathered up the dogs, especially Lindie, as he wasn't sure if she would chase or not.

Everyone now safely in the FJ, Bud was soon dropping down into the Yellow Cat, where instead of turning left like he and Cal had done, he turned right, taking the road to the Ringtail Mine.

Thinking about the letter from the mailbox, he wondered when the pair had seen the woman from New York—it had to have been sometime yesterday, after he'd seen the writer in the cafe, since Hum and Cal had recovered her body earlier today.

But since Cal had said the coroner had indicated that her body had been out there for at least a day, that meant she'd had to have died the previous day, not long after she'd left the cafe, so the pair must've seen her right after she left Green River.

Bud had seen Jay out at the missile base the previous morning, so if he was involved, it had to be between then and when he'd gotten stuck, which was a pretty small window of time.

The timeline for all this seemed sketchy to Bud, and he made a note to himself to be sure to talk to Cal when the coroner's report came in. Something didn't quite add up—and that 911 call was puzzling, to say the least.

In the meantime, he'd head over to the mine, the sketch of the plant in hand, and see what he could find, if anything. And if he had time, he'd wander over to the Poison Strip and see if he could maybe round up a cup of coffee at the Yellow Cat Cafe, though he knew he really should get back to Green River before long.

He headed on down the rough road, the boys now asleep in the back. Lindie was ever alert in the front, her nose resting on Bud's shoulder, where she could look out while enjoying the comfort of his soft denim jacket.

Bud was sorry that the woman had died, yet he was glad to be out in the wilds of the Big Empty. He wondered what it would be like to live in a big city like New York, where there were no views of distant cliffs or big horizons.

And as he pulled over to take a photo of a colorful stand of purple vetch, or locoweed, a sadness came over him. The woman had hardly had a chance to see any of the country out here, yet alone to get a feel for its solitude and beauty. He felt she'd missed out on something rare—had been so close—but then her life had been tragically cut short.

He opened the FJ door and let the dogs out, then, taking the lens cap off his camera, got down on his knees to get a better shot of the vetch. Was this the Yellow Cat Preuss poisonvetch like in the sketch Cal had faxed? No, the plant had a dark calyx, not a yellow one.

It was then that he saw something on the ground, its yellow color contrasting with the purple flowers—it was a small notebook. And as Bud opened it, he saw it was filled, over and over, with nothing but the words *Rosalind Lee* written in ink.

He paused, then carefully put the small notebook into his pocket. Had someone intentionally left it there, maybe tossing it from their car as they drove by, or had the winds blown it in?

Bud looked around for tracks for awhile, then, finding nothing, called the dogs back into the FJ, then again headed for the Ringtail Mine.

# 10

---

Bud had always loved desert wildflowers, many which had delicate richly-colored blooms that one would never guess came from the arid wildlands of the Big Empty.

It seemed that the harsher and dryer the area, the prettier the blooms, and Bud couldn't help but wonder if it didn't have something to do with a concerted survival effort to attract pollinators in an environment where life was so tenuous.

He knew that some plants had seeds that could lie dormant for decades and then quickly spring to life with a small amount of water. The region typically got less than 10 inches of moisture a year, much of which either came all at once in the monsoon season and quickly ran off or came in winter in the form of snow.

As he drove along, Bud could see more locoweed in bloom, a plant that was poisonous to ungulates like sheep, horses, and cattle. It seemed like the herds of pronghorn antelope that lived out there either were immune to it or knew better than to eat it.

He knew that technically they weren't antelope, but all the locals called them that, and using the term pronghorn was a sure sign you were from other parts.

He often saw the yellow gazelle-like animals with their white rumps out in the Big Empty, and he knew they preferred the wide open spaces, as their main defenses were their keen eyesight and swift movement. Their main predators were coyotes and golden eagles, which would swoop down and take away the fawns.

He'd also occasionally found their horns in the desert sand, and he knew that the antelope was the only animal in the world to shed its horns every year as if they were antlers. He'd often heard them make a barking sound and sometimes even strange noises like some kind of large exotic bird.

As he drove along, Bud kept a close eye on the small masses of purple colors, for he was hoping to get some good photos. He was also hoping to find some Preuss poisonvetch like in the sketch, though he knew it looked so much like the other locoweed varieties that the only way he'd recognize it was if he saw a yellow calyx.

He thought back to the description of the saguaro, Joshua tree, and locoweed in the mystery Howie had read to him and again wondered what had happened to its author. He knew that even though this barren desert landscape had its own beauty, it could be unforgiving for those who visited without proper preparation. Why had Marie Lee come out here? Did she know she would die?

Bud could now see the ruins of the Ringtail Mine in the distance and checked his GPS, the coordinates indicating he should stop near a small wash not far ahead.

He pulled over, the dogs now awake and excited. He could see where a vehicle had parked a dozen feet or so off the road, and he knew from the size of the tracks it had to be the little red roadster. The tracks were now partly obliterated by others that Bud suspected belonged to Hum and Cal's truck, as well as Tex Tanner's tow truck.

Bud parked and grabbed his camera, leaving the dogs inside the FJ, windows down a bit, much to their disappointment. He didn't want them out and about and possibly obliterating any evidence. He would take them for a hike on down by the mine later when he was done.

He stopped for a moment to gaze at the red cliffs of the national park which formed the distant southern edge of the Yellow Cat. The wide-open scenery was spectacular, and he recalled an old miner telling him that out here on a clear day you could see way past tomorrow.

He could indeed see clear to the green highlands of Pinion Mesa to the east over in Colorado, as well as the distinct point of Mt. Elliot jutting up from the Bookcliffs to the northwest over by Green River. And of course, the Salt Mountains stood above everything in their laccolithic majesty to the southeast, still wearing their white caps from the recent winter's snows, the front part of the range in Utah and the back trailing off into deep canyons and high plateaus in Colorado, places with names like Sewemup Mesa, where rustlers once hid cattle and altered their brands.

Bud now again felt a sadness, knowing Marie Lee would never see this view again. He wished he was out here on other business, or actually, on no business at all, for knowing she'd died nearby gave him a deep sense of regret, even though he hadn't known her.

He preferred to come out into the Big Empty to wander with the dogs and forget such tales of woe, not to try to figure out the where and why and how of such tales. But he knew it was part of his job, and Hum and Cal had done him a number of favors, so he didn't mind giving them a little of his time in return.

He now found a trail of tracks leading from the road and was soon following, figuring they would lead to where Hum and Cal had found the body. The tracks soon stopped at a spot near a large rock that appeared to have fallen eons ago from the rocky ridge above, and it was there that Bud indeed found an indentation in the dirt that indicated someone had been lying there in the shade.

Examining the tracks more closely, he could see that three different sizes of shoes had made them, which fit with the number of people that had been there. One set was smaller and lighter, the size a small person would make, and ended at the depression.

He now started back toward the road, again examining the tracks, noting that only two of the sets headed back and were somewhat deeper, as if they now weighed more. They had to be Hum and Cal's, and he figured they sank a little deeper into the dirt because they were now carrying Marie.

Now wanting to fiddle with something, Bud reached into his jacket pocket only to find he'd left his harmonica at home. He didn't really understand why, but he needed to fiddle to be able to think, and the harmonica had served him well ever since he'd found it—he was now even getting to be pretty proficient on it.

He sat on a large rock, suddenly longing to be back home in Green River at his cozy bungalow, sitting on the back porch drinking coffee and watching the dogs play. It was rare that the open expanses of the desert did this to him, and he knew it had to do with the woman's death.

But as he sat there, he slowly became aware that someone or something was slowly creeping up on him from behind the rocks, something that was now making a strange buzzing sound as it got closer and closer.

He froze, not sure what to do, now aware that his Ruger was still in its holster where he'd left it on his bed back at home, along with his harmonica, and like the antelope, all he had for his defense was his wits—and given their current condition, he felt he might be in a little bit of trouble.

# 11

Bud turned slowly to find a pair of antelope gazing at him from no more than 10 feet away, ears forward as if asking him just what in hellsbells he was doing out in their territory.

He'd had antelope come close like this before, but only when he was in his FJ, and he'd always assumed they hadn't realized there was a human inside. They'd even come up and scraped their teeth on its hood as if to see if it was edible.

He sat perfectly still, wanting to take their photo, yet knowing that raising his camera would frighten them away. They now inched closer, tenuously, as if they knew that their curiosity could get them in trouble and yet were unable to quell it.

They were now close enough to touch, and Bud felt a sense of wonder at being so close to the creatures, for he could now smell their earthy scent, as well as feel their breath on his face.

One suddenly snorted, the sound scaring the bejeebers out of Bud, making him jump, and the pair turned and took off running in one stride, their cloven hooves kicking dirt in Bud's face.

He did manage to get a shot with his camera, and looking at it later, Bud felt it was kind of artsy—two white fuzzy rumps flying through the air with brown dirt clods everywhere in front of a nice stand of red Indian paintbrush that made a contrasting blurry crimson bokeh background. When he showed the photo to Wilma Jean, she couldn't quite figure out what it was, though she said she liked the colors.

Something about seeing the antelope broke the tension, and Bud now felt his old sense of being at home in the desert. He knew he wasn't finished with the business at hand, but he could now maybe forget the more sorrowful part of it and enjoy where he was a little more.

He stuck his hand in his pocket from habit, looking again for his harmonica to fiddle with, then had to laugh at himself. He was out in the Yellow Cat, for crying out loud, one of the most prolific rock-hounding sites in all of Utah, a place littered with colorful specimens of agate, chert, jasper, and even petrified wood. It wouldn't be long before he could find an object worthy of his fiddling, if he'd just take the time to look around.

He walked along, taking photos of wildflowers, studying the ground for more clues, and soon found a piece of what looked to be some kind of deep-red flint with rough edges. It was about the size of a small piece of Dentine gum, something Bud was quite familiar with, as it had been his go-to when he'd quit smoking years ago.

The piece had been flint-knapped into an elongated triangle with serrated edges and a sharp point on one end, the other end being flat with notches where one could tie it onto a stick using a strip of hide. It appeared he'd found a small arrowhead, a completely intact bird point, and he could tell by its patina that it had to be quite old.

He'd found lots of native workings during his wanderings— points of various sizes, awls, scrapers, and even manos and metates— but he'd always left them. He knew that collecting such antiquities was frowned upon by archaeologists, as it removed the prehistory from an area, but this one he would keep, as he was desperate.

He'd mark the location where he found it with his GPS and take it to the local BLM office up in Price next time he was there, or heck, maybe even bring it back out here where it belonged, but for now he needed it to help him solve a possible murder, and who could argue with good intentions like that?

He also knew that right now his heart was more into photographing flowers than solving a murder, so he was going to need all the help he could get.

# 12

---

Bud now began wandering in wider and wider circles, looking for any clues as to what had gone on, fiddling with the little bird point as he went, feeling much more centered.

He now saw tracks coming from the direction of the road, and he began following them. These were identical to the ones by where Marie's body had been, Bud noted. As he walked along next to them, he spied something that looked out of place, a dark spot against the tan clay.

Walking over to it, he found a small makeshift fire ring with ashes still in it. He knew the fire had to be recent, for the spring winds in the Yellow Cat could be fierce, and the ashes looked undisturbed—in fact, a few partially burned sheets of paper were still inside the ring. Bud pulled them out and examined them.

If he were to make a list of things he was likely to find in a fire ring, it wouldn't include sheet music, yet there it was, and he could even make out some of the words:

> His object all sublime,
> He will achieve in time,
> To let the punishment fit the crime.

The words seemed vaguely familiar, but he couldn't quite place them. Did they have anything to do with someone being murdered? It was all very strange, he thought, fiddling again with the bird point.

It didn't particularly look like the kind of fire one would start to keep warm, as the fire ring wasn't big enough, and the shallow ashes showed there hadn't been much to it. Was someone trying to burn the music to be rid of it? Was it a sacrifice to the music gods?

Bud was baffled, and he snapped several photos. He also photographed the tracks, then followed them as they headed back to the road. Had someone come out here just to start a small fire, then gone back? Were they trying to hide something by burning it?

He now began randomly wandering, fiddling with the bird point, looking for more clues. He was about ready to call it quits and go take the dogs out when he came upon a strange track that looked like someone had dragged a small artist's paintbrush through the dirt with tiny pinpoints along each side. He knew he was looking at the track of a giant desert centipede, a black and red fuzzy centipede that had a bite like a scorpion, though non-poisonous.

He hadn't seen many, since they were nocturnal, but he did recall seeing one by flashlight over in the San Rafael Swell that was a good foot long. They were typically smaller, but the name referred to how large they could potentially get, and this one looked to be big, based on its track.

Intrigued, Bud followed the track for quite a ways, wondering if he'd find its hole, but instead, the track led into a small outcropping of rocks. Now looking up, he saw a beautiful mass of purple locoweed, and pleasantly surprised, walked over to take photos.

Working his way around the plants, which made for some nice pictures the way they backed up to the picturesque yellow rocks, Bud was now surprised to find where several had been dug up. He figured some small animal like a ground squirrel had been digging, but when he walked around to the other side, he found more tracks, exactly like the ones that had led to Marie's body.

Someone had walked to the locoweed, someone with a small footprint, and he suspected it was Marie. Parts of several plants lay on the ground, as if she'd pulled them up and then dropped them, maybe looking for a better specimen.

Bud now took the fax from his pocket and studied it. The plants looked the same as the sketch of Preuss poisonvetch, with purple flowers rising from a woody base. He smelled one, and sure enough, it had the faint odor of garlic, which the description had said was from selenium.

Now looking closer, he could see that the calyx was indeed yellow. Was he looking at the endemic subspecies that grew only in the Yellow Cat? He was sure of it.

He carefully took several photos. Maybe someone in Green River could identify it for certain, but he was sure it was Preuss poisonvetch.

He now began following the tracks. They led farther down the outcrop to where a large juniper grew against the rocks, and it now appeared that someone had sat under it, for Bud could see where some leaves from the locoweed had fallen, presumably from one of the plants they were carrying.

Now, as Bud looked closer, he could see something in the shade of the tree, something that looked out of place. It took his eyes a moment to become acclimated to the shadows, but he soon made out something small and unnaturally white.

He at first thought he'd found a bone or even another arrowhead, but he soon realized he was looking at what appeared to be a small white ceramic mortar and pestle! All around it lay pieces of locoweed.

Had whoever pulled up the plants carried one over here to the shade, then ground part of it using the mortar and pestle? If so, why?

He carefully picked up the mortar, looking into its small bowl, where he saw something finely ground into a paste.

What struck him most was the paste's color—it was the most ethereal yellow he'd ever seen, maybe similar to what artists called saffron. He again recalled the description of the locoweed—*a subspecies with a beautiful yellow calyx*—along with the words—*What color!*—written alongside the sketch.

Apparently Marie had seen a photo somewhere and was struck

by the color, and for good reason, he thought, for it truly was beautiful and unique, the yellow having a very subtle hint of orange.

Bud carefully put the mortar and pestle in an evidence bag from his pocket, then sat for awhile in silence, not sure what to make of everything.

Why would Marie come all the way out here, apparently for a plant that grew only in the Yellow Cat, if not for some important reason? To Bud, going to all that trouble just to grind a calyx to see its color didn't make sense. Had she ingested some of the plant and poisoned herself?

Finally getting up, he again followed the tracks, which led straight back to the road where it looked like the roadster had been parked. She must have then walked to the place where Hum and Cal had found her, Bud figured.

Finally getting into the FJ where the dogs patiently waited, he drove on down the road toward the mine until he came upon a wide wash. He stopped and let the dogs out, wondering if Lindie would stay with them or run off, as it would be the first time he'd brought her out into the Big Empty with no leash.

They were soon walking down the sandy wash, the dogs stopping every so often to sniff under some bush or to dig, Lindie watching as if learning the ways of the land from seasoned desert dogs.

Bud fiddled with the bird point as they slowly wandered along, wondering if he would ever learn the mystery of what had happened to Marie Lee.

After awhile, he would load up the dogs and head back to Green River, for there wasn't really anything more he could do out there, at least not that he was aware of, and he needed to get back to the office.

# 13

---

It was the next morning, and Bud sat in the back booth at the Melon Rind, waiting for Heather to serve his breakfast. He wasn't sure where Maureen was, but he was hoping she'd finally given up and decided to stay home until the baby came.

He usually ate breakfast at home, saving the Melon Rind for lunch, but today he'd felt like getting out, especially since Wilma Jean was out doing another air-drop. For some reason, he was feeling like he needed to be out and about, doing something, though he wasn't sure what. He felt restless, and he knew it probably had to do with Marie's death and wanting to figure it all out.

He was now thinking about Lindie, and how she'd been such a good dog lately, especially the previous day out in the wash with the others, making no move to run off. He thought again about what Jay had said about her being a good search-and-rescue, or SAR, dog.

Maybe she would be good at SAR—she was certainly smart enough. He'd have to get online and see if he could research how to train her. The SAR team down in Radium had a certified SAR dog, and maybe they could help him out. Such a dog might come in handy, like yesterday when he was trying to find where Marie had gone.

He fiddled with the harmonica in his pocket, having retrieved it from where he'd left it on the bed the previous day, next to his gun. He began listening to the chatter around him, the cafe almost full, guessing that most of the customers were rockhounds here for the Green River Rock and Mineral Festival.

He'd seen various signs around town welcoming the attendees, signs like the one at the Westwinds that read, "Welcome Rockhounds," and one at the museum that read, "Welcome Dirty Dogs," which he assumed was the name of some rockhound club.

He knew that some rockhounds just enjoyed the collecting, but others cut and polished the rocks they found with saws and grinders and various lapidary equipment, making cabochons for belt buckles, bolo ties, and rings, sometimes even selling them. It was a hobby that Bud could understand well, as he himself had a small pile of rocks by his garage.

The rock show wasn't all that big, especially compared to the one in Radium or the really big one in Tucson, but it had a nice variety and attracted what Bud considered to be good down-to-earth people.

Now the fellow in the booth nearest his, a middle-aged man wearing a red and white baseball jacket, was holding something up to the light coming through the cafe window, saying, "Hawk, you're the luckiest dog south of the North Pole to dig up something like this. I really like how the carnelian delineates the orange from the white."

Bud couldn't quite make out what it was, though it appeared to be some kind of rock.

The guy named Hawk answered, "Yeah, I always get lucky in this country. Green River's one of my favorite places to hound, and you wouldn't believe some of the stuff I've found."

Bud now heard someone at a nearby table with a half-dozen people at it say, "Well, Snuffy, I have just as much fun as someone who knows what they're doing. Last year, I was out in the Yellow Cat and found some of that petrified redwood, a rare limb cast. I gave it a nice flat lap polish on one side and made a display stand and man, is it pretty."

A woman's voice answered, "Yellow Cat Flats is my go-to for agate. Always good stuff there."

Now someone else said, "You got that right, Celestite. There's a fellow over in Grand Junction who did a nice book on Yellow Cat redwood, his name's Frank Daniels. It's full of really nice color photos, but a tad expensive. I told my wife I wanted it for my birthday, but she wasn't about to spend that much on me. Got me a rock hammer instead, though I already had one."

"Can't ever have too many rock hammers," the woman commented.

"What you can't have too much of is that pigeon-blood agate," someone said. "That stuff really makes some nice cabs. Ira had some he sold."

The fellow Bud guessed was named Snuffy replied, "There's lots of that off the Floy exit, though it's getting hunted out. But there's still some at the Squeeze."

"Where's that?" asked Ira.

Snuffy replied, "You know where Black Dragon is? Well, there's a little dirt road that takes off on the other side of the freeway to the south. It comes out by the Hatt Ranch on the road to Hanksville, goes through the Squeeze."

Now Celestite added, "Lots of grape agate there, agate pseudomorphs after barite. Agate-filled mudball geodes, too. Nice stuff. But you gotta be careful out there, no place to winch off of, so you don't want to get stuck."

A gray-haired older fellow who'd been silent until now said, "I've never been stuck, only momentarily detained."

Snuffy snorted, "What's more fun than being bogged in a remote place? Besides, you stimulate the economy when you get stuck."

The gray-haired guy asked, "How so?"

"Tow trucks," Snuffy said.

Ira now said, "Never had to call one. I always dig myself out. Those boards are the cat's meow. Always carry a set."

Snuffy asked, "What kind of boards you talkin' about? Two by fours? Sideboards? Outboards? Ouija boards?"

Now Celestite added, "I've never been stuck, but I occasionally have been unable to maintain forward momentum. But you know, Snuffy, the only thing that keeps you looking smart is the carefully managed lack of evidence to the contrary."

"What's that supposed to mean?" Snuffy asked.

Ira replied, "It means you only do stupid things when no one's looking."

Celestite said, "Some of us could argue that, but hey, what say we get going. It's a bit of a drive to Yellow Cat and time's a-wasting. I want to get back this evening in time for that geologist's talk about uranium."

"We could go rockhound out at the old missile base and be rocket-hounds," Snuffy laughed.

"Hey, any of you been out in the Yellow Cat and heard a strange noise?" Ira asked, ignoring Snuffy.

"What strange noise? What's it sound like?" Celestite asked.

"Kind of like a combination of someone singing and a bull bellowing. I heard it yesterday."

Bud was now all ears, thinking of the letter from the fellow called Jasper. He took it from his jeans-jacket pocket and again read:

*We've been hearin' somethin' strange out in the distance. You might wanna tell the Holyoaks one of their bulls is lost out here.*

Bud had thought they were just imagining things, or maybe a bull really was lost out there, but now he wasn't so sure.

As the rockhounds gathered their jackets and left the cafe, Bud thought of Jay Landowska and his I-SING plates. Was he out in the backcountry singing again? Was that what people were hearing? Bud hadn't seen him since he and Cal had got him unstuck. Did he know his ex-wife was dead?

Bud now felt like he needed to talk to Hum and Cal. Maybe it was time to go back to the office and make a few phone calls, plus he needed to get the mortar and pestle to them, as he was sure it was some kind of evidence.

His breakfast finished, he left a tip for Heather, then walked to the cafe door as a small skinny guy at the cafe counter was saying to his companion, "I used to go out and hike around, then come back and write it up, but anymore I just write it up without even going out. Google Earth. Pretty easy job, in my opinion."

Bud frowned, not sure what the fellow was talking about, then headed on out the door. He'd go see if Howie was home before heading back to the office. Maybe he'd have something interesting to relate from *The Last Opera Show*.

## 14

Bud sat in the wooden swing on the front porch of Howie and Maureen's old farm house, watching the campers at the state park across the road as they cooked hotdogs, pitched tents and horseshoes, and did all the things that people out for a weekend do.

He was waiting for Howie, who had gone inside to get the mystery, eager to bring Bud up to date on the plot.

The little white bunny that Howie had rescued and named Little Bun was contentedly grazing in the front yard, which Howie had secured so the rabbit couldn't escape. Bud had left Lindie in his FJ, not sure how she would react to the rabbit.

Howie soon came out the front door, handing Bud a tall glass of Old Man Green's watermelon spritzer, then sat down next to him and opened the book.

"We had a really busy day at the drive-in, Sheriff," Howie said. "Maureen and Heather are running it right now, giving me a little break, but I need to get back soon. But this book is turning out to be pretty interesting. I can hardly put it down. I know you want to know what it's about, given that it's by that woman they just found. Any clues on that yet?"

Bud nodded his head no as Howie continued.

"Anyway, the P.E. has been hired by some wealthy widow who drives a Maserati to figure out why her elderly father is acting so strange. The old guy lives in a big mansion on a hill, kind of this Gothic place, and he keeps telling everyone he's turning into a werewolf, but nobody believes him. Listen to this."

Howie began reading.

*I studied the old man, then said, "You were telling me that you were turning into a werewolf. Remember?"*

*The old man was surprised. "All the interesting things going on in this world, you still want to hear about that?"*

*"Yes sir, I'd like to know," I replied.*

*"You're thinking the old man is nuts just because he knows he's turning into a werewolf? Well, boy, you'll see. I was there that night looking at the moon from my balcony and all of a sudden there was a growling in my throat that I couldn't hold back. And you know what? I looked out there from that balcony and started howling like a big old timber wolf, and I felt for the first time that I belonged to something, to the timber wolves. I felt wild. It was fantastic. I'm going to sell everything I own—the big Rolls Royce, my mansion—and move to Yellowstone. I now know where I belong for the first time in my life."*

Bud grinned. "Howie, I don't think one can actually move to Yellowstone, unless you work there. And Yellowstone calls them gray wolves, though I guess they're probably the same as timber wolves."

Howie replied, "I know, I know, it's just like that saguaro and stuff, but the plot's getting interesting, even though the writer doesn't seem to research much. You know, Sheriff, sometimes this book seems like two different people wrote it. It goes back and forth in style, but I'm kind of getting used to it."

"Well," Bud said, "That would make sense if she plagiarized it like the article said she did. Maybe she just changed the parts she wanted without really integrating it all together."

"I just don't understand why she would plagiarize it in the first place," Howie said with concern. "Surely she knew she'd get caught, especially since her sister's a famous mystery writer."

Bud thought for a moment, sipping his spritzer, then said, "Howie, you may be on to something here. Maybe she wasn't really interested in being a writer at all, but was instead trying to get some message across."

"What kind of message?"

"I don't know. But just keep reading the book, and maybe you'll come up with something. I suspect that, since her sister was famous, she had connections and was able to get a prestigious publisher."

"But wouldn't they know the book was plagiarized?"

"Not if her sister hadn't yet had hers published. But maybe her sister did give her permission to use it."

"Then why pull the book?"

"I don't know, Howie. But keep checking it out."

Howie continued reading as Bud watched the campers across the street. Finally, Howie said, "This part's kind of interesting. Listen to this."

*The Hotel Irvine's dining room was one of those places where a tuxedoed maître d' meets you at the door simply to sneer at you, then another tuxedoed man comes up behind him and takes you to your table.*

*Jill Thaddeus was already there at a table in a private corner. She wore an expensive looking slate-blue cocktail dress with a diamond necklace and matching earrings. Her auburn hair was pulled back, held up by a diamond brooch.*

*I slid into the chair across from her and said, "I went and saw your father."*

*She asked, "Did you see his bats?"*

*"Not yet, but I've been invited to," I replied.*

*She looked down into her champagne glass, swirled the liquid around, then fluttered her eyelashes at me a few times.*

*I wasn't going to fall for it. Instead, I said, "There's something that bothers me. What if he really is turning into a werewolf?"*

*Her shoulders slumped.*

*"Your father seems to have a few screws loose," I continued. "But to tell you the truth, I like the old guy. He says you're trying to take his money. Why would he say that?"*

*She was speechless, then recovered. "That's the most ridiculous thing Father has come up with yet," she said, dabbing a crocodile tear from her eye with the dinner napkin. "And if anyone's trying to get his money, it's my ex-husband. He and Father sang together at the Met, and Father trusts him. I have evidence that he wants me dead and out of the way."*

*"Why did you divorce him?" I asked.*

*"He's a very dangerous man. He likes snakes. And besides, I got tired of hearing opera all day, especially Gilbert and Sullivan. But now he's in a motorcycle gang."*

Howie now stopped reading and said, "Sheriff, I think she *is* trying to get his money and everything else is just a ruse. But do you suppose this has anything to do with the writer who just died? Was someone trying to get *her* money?"

"Howie, I don't even know if she had any money."

"What's her name, anyway, Bud?"

"It's on the cover—Marie Lee."

"Oh, of course," Howie said, now looking at the book's cover. "*The Last Opera Show* by Marie Lee. But who's her sister?"

Bud now finished the last of his spritzer and leaned back in the swing, fiddling with his harmonica and thinking. Someone across the street had brought in a huge Holiday Rambler motor home and was trying to get it into a spot that looked like it was meant for a tent.

Finally, he answered, "Howie, I'm not sure. I've been a little lax with my research, just like Marie Lee or whoever actually wrote that book was with hers. I've been thinking it's not really my case, since it's down in Hum's territory, but those guys are so busy, maybe I should get a little more involved."

Howie was silent for awhile, then said, "Well, Sheriff, I'm a little busy right now, too, but you know if you need my help I'm here for you."

"I know that, Howie," Bud said, standing. "And I appreciate it. I just don't really have any idea where to start with this one—it's got me a bit stumped."

Howie also stood. "I need to get back to the drive-in, but it seems to me you'll figure it out given enough time. You always do, Sheriff."

Bud nodded, then walked out the gate, careful to close it tight so Little Bun couldn't escape, wondering if Marie Lee had been murdered for her money.

It would make more sense if she had still been married to Jay, as he would then stand to inherit whatever she had, but he'd said they were divorced. And where the heck was he, anyway? Had he gone back to New York?

Bud thought of the mortar and its contents, still in an evidence bag in his office, and he knew it was time to give Hum and Cal a call.

But first, he wanted to make a couple of phone calls on behalf of Lindie, the little Carolina dingo. He headed back to his office, Lindie riding in the passenger seat at his side, watching for rabbits.

## 15

---

Bud leaned back in the big chair in his office, sipping coffee, having just gotten off the phone. He'd been talking to Jody, the team leader for the search-and-rescue dogs group over in Colorado, who'd told him, "A SAR dog needs to be driven and have high energy, which is why we usually have working breed dogs." She'd been really helpful, even inviting Bud to bring Lindie over for an assessment.

Bud had tried to get ahold of the SAR dog trainer down in Radium, but she was out of town with her dog Sasha on a mission, helping look for a missing Boy Scout up near Salt Lake.

Jody had told Bud quite a bit about SAR dogs, which he'd found interesting. First, she'd said that the dog needed a built-in prey or herding drive, and so far, Bud was pretty sure Lindie would qualify. But he was a bit worried about his training abilities, for Jody had also said that the training's not something you can do halfway, and that you needed to practice as much as possible and as often as possible.

Jody had a border collie named Angus, and she'd told Bud that Angus had participated in over two-dozen SAR outings in just the past year. She'd also told him that SAR dogs used one of two types of scent tracking: some dogs followed the scent of a person on the ground while others followed scents in the air. Bud wondered which Lindie would be.

He now noticed Lindie was staring at the ceiling, and, looking up, he saw a big daddy longlegs. Getting the broom, he took it outside, telling Lindie, "You're sure a good watchdog. Too bad you can't do more than watch, like take bugs outside." She looked at him as if she understood.

Now Bud's phone rang.

"Yell-ow," he answered.

"Bud, you in your office? I'm in town and would like to pick up that evidence you said you found out in the Yellow Cat. It's actually my day off, and I'm on my way up to Price to pick up a load of hay."

"Sure, Cal, come on by, but be careful you don't get run over by a rockhound. We're having our annual rock show, and they're everywhere."

"I did notice three or four vehicles on the streets rather than the usual one or two," Cal joked. "I'll be right there. Over."

Lindie greeted Cal at the door, and Bud handed him a cup of coffee, as well as the bag with the mortar and pestle.

"I'll send this right off," Cal said. "And thanks for going out there. I knew you'd do a more thorough job than we could. It seems like there's always some kind of emergency or other these days around Radium. Too many tourists. Hum needs another deputy. You interested in coming back?"

Bud smiled as Cal continued. "I got a call yesterday from one of the park rangers. They had a half-dozen or more calls come in saying they heard someone yelling for help, and it was coming from the area down by Salt Wash. The park says they couldn't find anyone, and one of the rangers I talked to says he heard it, and it actually sounded more like a bull bellowing."

Bud now thought back to what the rockhounds had said. "You know, Cal, I overheard some people talking about the same thing in the cafe yesterday."

"What do you think it could be?" Cal asked.

"I keep thinking about that opera guy singing up in the rocks. I'm not saying that's what it is, but it might be."

"Interesting," Cal mused, shaking his head. "He must have a pretty good set of pipes. What would he be doing out there?"

"I don't know, just singing, I guess. Maybe he's stuck again."

"Well, if so, he's on his own this time. Maybe those two squatters out there can help him out. But say, Bud, I have something I want you to hear. You know me and Hum are both amateur radio operators, HAMs. I have a nice radio shack out behind my house with a 40-foot dipole antenna, and I can pick up quite a bit. Anyway, I was listening to the local chatter last evening when I heard about some show that was supposed to come on at seven. Now, Bud, you know HAM radio is nothing like broadcast radio, it's totally for communications and nothing remotely resembling entertainment, unless you call a bunch of old guys talking about the weather entertainment. It's totally illegal to tie up a frequency. You're supposed to pause every three minutes or so, give your call letters, then let someone else have a chance."

Cal now took a small recorder from his pocket, saying, "So when I heard about this so-called show, I got out my little recorder here and decided to record what was going on. HAM radio frequencies are critical to emergency communications, and shows are not allowed. So anyway, kick back and listen to this."

Bud leaned back in his chair, ready to listen, Lindie asleep at his feet, her head on his foot as he sipped his coffee.

# 16

___

As Cal hit the play button, a raspy voice immediately came on, and Cal paused it, saying, "This guy calls himself Jasper, and his buddy, who'll come on soon, is Leon. I timed it, and they tied up the frequency for over 20 minutes, which included some really bad banjo playing and our friend Jay singing, though I didn't record that part. OK, here goes."

*CQ, CQ, and hello out there to all you HAM radio folks, and welcome to another espeedode of K-RAT Radio, that's K-R-A-T, comin' to you from the Cactus Rat Mine and the Yeller Cat Cafe out here on the Poison Strip, the most beautious place on Planet Earth.*

*First, here's the local news. The big headliner for today is that Yeller Cat Wash ran, and it ran real good. Me and Leon took my old army amblance over to the back road into the park so we could resupply, and we did real good over there, I can tell you that.*

Now another voice came on, one less raspy.

*I'm Leon, and we stocked up on some little goldfish crackers, cheese, gorp, and even a six pack of water. Jasper refused to believe that people would pay for water like that, but there it was right in front of his eyes. The nice thing about our borrowing is that the ravens get blamed for it.*

Jasper now continued.

*So anyway, we were tooling right along on our way home, until we came to where the wash was running, and there was even a nice waterfall there right by the road, tumbling over the rocks. We had to wait for three hours before we could cross, so we had ourselves a little picnic right there. It was actually kind of fun, until we realized we'd eaten up most of the stuff we'd borrowed from the campers at the park. So, it looks like we'll be taking another little trip over there pretty soon, unless some of you listeners decide to come on out to the Poison Strip, and if you do, bring pretty much anything good to eat you can think of. Or at the very least, don't lock your vehicles when you're out rockhounding.*

*But folks, we've been told that the FCC has a rule that you have to identify yourself every three minutes or so, so we're K-R-A-T, that's Kilo Romeo Alpha Tango. And the FCC also says you can't hog the frequency, so we're gonna unkey the mic so you can talk for a bit, then we'll go back to the show. OK, here's your chance to be a part of K-RAT radio, folks, so talk away.*

*<silence>*

*OK, enough of that, and okie dokie, the wash ran. And now we have a special treat for you, all the way from New York City. Yup, you heard me right, New York City. Folks, after some of my famous banjo pickin', we're gonna have us a little private concert by an opera singer who's agreed to sing us some Willy Nelson. Don't go away.*

Cal turned the recorder off, saying, "I ran out of tape, but I know that singer was our buddy Jay, as it sounded just like him. I just ordered a digital recorder, so maybe next time I can get it all. He sang a couple of Willy Nelson tunes—*Blue Eyes Crying in the Rain* and *On the Road Again*. He has a nice voice, though I prefer Willy's rendition."

Bud laughed, then said, "That's actually pretty entertaining, legal or not. And I had a hunch Jay was still out there. But it seems pretty obvious that they know they're breaking the FCC rules."

"Agreed," Cal replied. "I know these guys are just having some fun, and I'm actually really hesitant to turn them in, as I don't want to get them into trouble. But I'm thinking I might have a little talk with them next time I'm out there. They're tying up the frequency, and there may come a time when that frequency is needed for someone's emergency call—and who knows, that emergency call might be on their behalf."

"What I find amazing," Bud said, "Is that they actually confessed to stealing from campers at the park. I think you guys have your thieves right there."

"It's very possible," Cal replied. "Actually, it's very probable. I have no idea why they would say something like that on the air. Surely they know they're going to get busted for it. And that makes me wonder if they're really the ones doing it. They may be using a little, what's it called?"

"Poetic license?"

"Yeah, a little poetic license to entertain their listeners. It's possible they don't know that there really are thefts going on in the park. I know that I personally would never admit to something like that on the air if I were really doing it. Or even if I weren't. But what the ranger said about the tracks matches, if they're driving an old army ambulance like that guy Jay told us when we got him unstuck. But anyway, I need to get going. I borrowed a friend's flatbed and I need to go load a couple of tons of hay."

Cal stood, and Bud followed him to the door, saying somewhat hesitantly. "Glad you stopped by. But Cal, there's something I need to ask you."

"Ask away."

"I know the Yellow Cat's not my jurisdiction, but I also know how busy you guys are. Nothing much ever happens around here, and I'm willing to put some time and effort into solving this case as long as it's OK by you and Hum. I sure don't want to interfere if you fellows have a handle on it."

"Handle on it?" Cal guffawed. "We haven't even hardly had the time to think about it. I know I can speak for Hum when I say we'd be very appreciative to have your help. In fact, I'll designate you the lead investigator right here and now. Anything we find out will be run by you first, including the results of what's in this bag."

"Thanks, Cal. Any word back yet on the coroner's report?"

"Not yet, but I'll call you when it comes in. In the meantime, have at it. I know Hum will be willing to cover any gas and expenses you incur, just keep track."

Bud showed Cal out the door, relieved. He was beginning to feel a sense of ownership of the case, probably because he felt like he knew Jay and had seen the writer when she was still alive, plus he was reading her book vicariously through Howie.

He now knew for sure that Jay was probably back out in the Yellow Cat, and he also knew it would be the perfect place to start training Lindie to be a SAR dog.

## 17

---

Bud started a new pot of coffee, relieved that he would now be the lead investigator on Marie's case. This gave him the freedom he needed to proceed, and he was now beginning to feel like he was in a better position to solve the case anyway, simply because Green River was more the center of the coming and goings out there.

He started playing tug of war with Lindie, using an old towel, when he remembered that the rock show was sponsoring a talk by geologist Shorty Doyle, PhD. on Yellow Cat uranium, and it was something Bud for sure didn't want to miss.

Shorty was now retired, but even though he was originally from Green River, he'd been a crackerjack geologist with his own TV show up in Canada, and Bud had Lindie because of Shorty, as he'd brought the little dog to Bud from the Yukon.

Shorty was currently dating the high-school science teacher, Cassie Rose, a good geologist in her own right, and Bud suspected it wouldn't be long until they made their relationship formal. In fact, Maureen had told him she'd heard them talking marriage one evening at the Melon Rind Cafe, though she made Bud promise to not say anything to anyone.

Bud figured if Maureen knew about it, it would soon be public knowledge, for she was friends with Wanda, who wasn't just the town's mail carrier, but also its news carrier.

Bud took Lindie out to the bungalow, fed her and the boys, then gave them each a chewie in the back yard, where they could lounge around on the grassy lawn, guarding things from rabbits until Bud got back.

Soon at the museum, he opened the door into the small auditorium, then quickly closed it behind him so as to not disturb anyone, for he was late and Shorty had already begun his talk. He could see the room was almost full, and he slipped into a seat in the very back, just behind the woman and fellow he recognized from the cafe as Celestite and Ira.

Shorty was saying, "And as you all know, lots of dinosaurs have been found in both the Yellow Cat member and the Morrison formation. The Yellow Cat is the bottom of the Cedar Mountain formation, and immediately overlies the Morrison. At the contact between the two, you'll often find smoothly polished pebbles thought to be gastroliths, which are pebbles ingested by dinosaurs to aid in digestion, just like many modern birds have, which are evolved from the avian dinosaurs. But today's lecture is not about dinosaurs, but rather, about uranium."

Bud studied the crowd. He recognized a number of Green Riverites, as well as people he figured were probably visiting rockhounds. He was surprised to see Mrs. Jensen sitting next to Frosty and Eldon a few rows up, for as far as he knew, she'd never shown any interest in geology.

Shorty continued, "Now, I'm pretty sure you all can easily recognize the Morrison formation, especially the colorful stripes of the Brushy Basin member, and it's the main source for uranium on the Colorado Plateau, which holds some of the richest deposits in the world. In the 1940s, after the development of the atomic bomb, uranium became a valuable resource and the boom was on, and it hit this area hard. Lots of people came out here to prospect for uranium, hoping to strike it rich."

The crowd seemed intrigued, and Shorty went on.

"One of the main uranium districts on the plateau was the Thompson District, which included the Yellow Cat area. If you've ever noticed the big black pyramid just outside of Green River, not far from the museum here, you can say you've seen where the tailings from the uranium reduction plant here were capped to keep the radioactive waste from blowing all over creation, though since they capped them a number of years after the boom, they may have been a bit late. But all the uranium in this district comes from lenses of sandstone that make up ancient river channels. Now how exactly does that work, you may be asking."

Bud was wondering exactly that, and Shorty, as if reading his mind, nodded in his direction, though Bud didn't think he could actually see him in the dark.

"OK, I'll tell you. Uranium originates in volcanic rocks, but is widely disseminated and impossible to get at in any quantity. Now, I'm going to greatly simplify this, but what you need is a mechanism where these radioactive elements are leached from their source beds and precipitated into bigger deposits that can be mined. Well, we have exactly that right here in the Colorado Plateau in the form of ancient river channels that have, though time, become sandstone conduits."

Bud was now feeling sleepy, but he wanted to know about the area's geology, so he pulled his harmonica from his pocket and began running his fingers up and down the reeds, trying to stay awake. He wondered where he'd left the little bird point, hoping he hadn't lost it.

"So, we have chemically rich fluids that slowly, over millions of years, concentrate there in the sandstones, and eventually you have enough uranium ore to mine. Black pitchblende and yellow carnotite are the two main uranium ores. Maybe you've come upon a big bright yellow fossilized log out in Yellow Cat country. These trees hold some of the richest ore."

Bud was getting sleepier and sleepier. He again looked around the room, noticing Hawk and his companion from the cafe sitting across the aisle, as well as Junkyard Goldie and Old Man Green a few rows up. Everyone else looked interested and engaged, but he was having trouble keeping his eyes open.

Shorty was now pointing to a slide projected on a big screen behind him.

"Now, in the Yellow Cat region, you have a large fold created by salts deep below dissolving and collapsing. This is called the Salt Valley anticline. Most of the uranium deposits contained in the Yellow Cat area occur along the northeast flank of this anticline, near the boundary of the national park. And that's where you'll find all the old mines."

Bud now began tapping his feet against the chair ahead of him in an attempt to stay awake, but quit when its occupant turned and scowled at him.

"I'm sure you've all heard of Charlie Steen, known as the Uranium King for finding one of the richest uranium deposits in the world, and he also knew about anticlines trapping ores, since he was a geologist. His mine, Mi Vida, was found on the southwest flank of the Lisbon Valley salt anticline. People thought he was nuts to drill there, but he knew his geology."

Bud now imagined he could hear bees or something droning, and though he was still listening, everything was becoming muddled.

"Why anticlines? Salt anticlines act to concentrate uranium ore. Rising groundwater migrated upward along the flanks of the salt anticlines toward the axes, and there the uranium was precipitated out of the water."

Now Bud slid downward, resting his head against the back of his seat, still listening.

"And as the water rises, one can easily hear singing coming from the rocks, for the soluble nature of the sandstone makes the rock vibrate and shake, and this in turn creates sounds like a bull bellowing, and sometimes one can even hear stanzas from famous operas, like the Barber of Seville."

The next thing Bud knew, Shorty was shaking his shoulder.

"I know I can get boring, Bud, but could you at least sit in the corner where nobody will see you sleeping?"

Shorty laughed, and Bud could see they were the last ones left in the auditorium.

Bud jumped to his feet, embarrassed, then began mumbling something about sound vibrating through the rocks to show Shorty he'd been listening, but caught himself when he realized he'd been dreaming.

He said, "It was a fascinating lecture, Shorty. I just need a cup of coffee."

"Well, come on over to my place and I'll make you one," Shorty replied. "I have something I've been wanting to show you, anyway."

"I'll meet you there," Bud said, finally awake, wondering if what Shorty had to show him had anything to do with falling asleep during his talks, which he had also occasionally done when Shorty had been his high-school science teacher many years back.

Bud was soon in his FJ and following Shorty's old Ford pickup out to the farm Shorty had inherited from his parents and whose fields butted up to Bud and Wilma Jean's melon farm.

Bud wondered what Shorty had been up to since coming back from the Yukon, and now he'd find out, he mused, pulling into Shorty's drive.

# 18

"This is the house I grew up in," Shorty was telling Bud, "But my parents wouldn't recognize it now. Cassie and I have been working really hard on getting it fixed up. What do you think?"

Shorty had been leasing the farm to a local guy until recently deciding to return to Green River, and Bud had noted that the place had been getting more and more run down. It was one of the original farm houses in the area, and it reminded Bud somewhat of his and Wilma Jean's bungalow, as it was surrounded by a big grassy lawn, heirloom roses and honeysuckle, and big cottonwoods, an oasis in the hot summers.

"We're going to paint the outside, now that the inside's done," Shorty continued. "But Bud, I don't really know what to do with it then. I was hoping you might have some ideas."

Walking inside, Bud was amazed at how the house had been transformed. He'd only been in it a couple of times, but he remembered it as being a typical old farm house, probably built at the turn of the 19th century, with peeling wallpaper and scuffed-up hardwood floors that needed refinishing. What he saw now could easily be in a fancy magazine—maybe not quite *Architectural Digest*, but close.

"I can't believe what you guys have done here," Bud said,

admiring the beautiful hand-crafted crown molding and refinished oak floors with their colorful thick Mexican-style rugs. The kitchen had all new appliances and a unique Saltillo tile that really brightened the place up, as well as a copper stove hood.

"Most of it was Cassie—she has good taste. But I think we've created a white elephant, Bud."

"A white elephant? How so?"

"Well, let me show you something."

Shorty went to an antique roll-top desk and took out a piece of paper, handing it to Bud.

Bud asked, "A marriage certificate from the courthouse over in Castle Dale? You guys got married?" He was surprised—not that they'd gotten married, but that they'd managed to keep it a secret in a small town like Green River.

"We got married shortly after I came back, Bud. We kind of just eloped. You know, I dated Cassie back at Stanford when she was my student, though it was on the hush hush then, even though she's not that much younger than me. Then she met the guy she ended up marrying and moved here, and I got a job with the Yukon Survey, and the rest is history. I'd been planning on retiring back here anyway, but when you told me her husband had been killed several years back in a farm accident, I told myself I wasn't going to let her get away this time."

"But why elope?" Bud asked, though he thought he knew the answer.

"Well," Shorty replied, "We didn't actually elope, we just went and got married at the courthouse. Neither of us is very traditional —we're geologists." Shorty laughed. "We just couldn't see having a big wedding and all, especially at our ages. That certificate is one of the things I wanted to show you, but the other is this view out here."

Shorty pointed out the kitchen window to a nice view of the hay fields that backed up to Bud's melon farm. Bud knew Shorty probably wouldn't ask him to come all the way out here just to show him the view, so he suspected something else was going on.

"I do like that view," Bud replied. He could see several cars in front of the Melon View B&B across the way, which his wife owned.

"Bud, I'm living out at Cassie's ranch with her now. I don't know what to do with this place. I was going to sell it after we fixed it all up, but I just can't do it. My great-grandparents settled this farm and built this house, and it has too many memories. My mom planted those honeysuckle bushes out there along the fence."

Shorty paused, hesitating, then said, "And now it's just too nice to be a rental. What I'm wondering is if you would want to lease it out. It would be easy for you to farm, being right next to your place, and maybe Wilma Jean would want to turn this into another B&B. Cassie and I are hoping to do some traveling, so we really don't want to be tied to it, and I don't want to lease it to just anyone, after fixing it all up. I'd give you some really good terms—you know we don't really need the money. You could keep it in hay, which isn't as much work as melons."

Bud was surprised. After being a lowly farm manager for the past few years, farms now seemed to be falling out of the sky. It hadn't been all that long since he and Wilma Jean had bought the melon farm, and Bud really liked the stability that came with owning property, even though it also involved a lot of work. They'd been like Shorty, suddenly having two places to stay, so they'd opted to stay in their bungalow on its two acres and turn the farm house into a B&B.

"I really appreciate the offer, Shorty, but I'm going to have to talk it over with Wilma Jean. What with all she's got going on, she doesn't have much spare time. I've got my hired hand, Kale, managing most of the farm, and his wife Molly pretty much runs the B&B, but with me being sheriff and all, we still keep pretty busy."

"I understand, Bud," Shorty replied, looking disappointed.

"I'm not saying no, Shorty. I just need to talk it over with Wilma Jean and make sure we could handle it. I'm not sure we're ready for a business empire. That would make two farms, two B&Bs, one cafe, one air catering business, and part of a bowling alley—plus my job as sheriff."

"Part of a bowling alley?"

"Wilma Jean traded part of it to Vern and Iris for her first airplane. It's working out really well so far, as Iris pretty much runs it. We don't make a lot off it, but we also don't have to do much, and Wilma Jean still owns the building."

"Sounds like a good plan to me, Bud. Say, I promised you a cup of coffee, and it's ready. What do you take?"

Bud grinned. "Any ice cream?"

"I think there's some chocolate in the freezer," Shorty replied.

"Hows about just some regular cream?" Bud asked.

Shorty and Bud took their coffee out onto the back patio and got comfortable in a pair of wicker chairs.

"You're not in a hurry, are you?" Shorty asked.

Bud replied, "No, and Shorty, I need to talk to you. You know we go back a bit, and I'm having some problems with a case I'm trying to solve. Howie's too busy to be a sounding board right now, and I really need to talk to someone who might give me some ideas as to what's going on."

"I'm not sure how much help I can be, Bud, but shoot."

Bud replied, "OK, but get comfortable, 'cause it's going to take awhile. See, there's this writer and this opera singer..."

"Did they walk into a bar together?" Shorty grinned.

Bud laughed, then proceeded to tell Shorty everything he knew about Marie Lee, Jay Landowska, and the Yellow Cat Cafe.

When he was done, Shorty was quiet for awhile, then said, "Bud, maybe it's time we go check out the Yellow Cat Cafe. First thing tomorrow morning?"

Bud nodded in agreement, told Shorty he'd talk to Wilma Jean that evening about the farm, then said goodbye and headed home.

## 19

Wilma Jean held out her hand, and Bud could see she had the little bird point he thought he'd lost.

She said, "This was on the kitchen counter. It looks like something you might not want to lose. Where did you find it? It's really pretty."

He grimaced at the thought of leaving such a treasure just anywhere. He'd been wondering where it was, and it was so tiny he figured he'd probably never see it again.

"I found it out in the Yellow Cat," he answered. "I was trying to figure out what happened to that writer."

"What writer?" Wilma Jean asked.

Bud sighed, but before he could answer, Wilma Jean said, "Oh, the one whose body they found. Are you taking on cases for Hum now? Isn't that his territory? We need to get back down there and have dinner with him and Peggy Sue. It's been too long."

Bud nodded his head in agreement as the little dachshund Pierre began tugging and chewing on his pant leg.

Wilma Jean continued. "I made you a nice cherry pie, hon, but you need to go easy on it. I'm noticing you're putting a little of that weight back on that you lost up in the Yukon. By the way, did you hear the news? Shorty and Cassie are getting married."

Bud grinned. For once, he was ahead of the Green River grapevine.

"They eloped. They're already married," he said.

"How do you know that?" Wilma Jean asked, surprised.

"Shorty told me."

"Well, how they kept that a secret is beyond me. But did you know Mrs. Jensen is dating Frosty Merriott?"

Bud laughed. "I've seen them together a couple of times. That would explain why we're not getting calls from her all the time about things like kids riding bikes across her lawn. Are they formally dating?"

"That's what Maureen told me. But I brought some tuna casserole home for dinner. Come have some while it's still warm."

"Tuna casserole?"

"It was today's special. The rockhounds love it. I call it Retro Tuna. I think most of them are stuck in the past, anyway."

Bud laughed as they sat down at the kitchen table, Pierre still dragging along on his pant leg. Hoppie and Lindie had already taken their places under the table, hoping Bud would slip them an occasional bite or two. Pierre now let go of Bud's pant leg so he could take his place, not wanting to miss out.

"We should just put a little table for them under ours," Wilma Jean nodded at the dogs.

Bud laughed, slipping them each a bite of casserole, then said, "It would probably be the civilized thing to do. We could get them a tablecloth with little biscuits printed on it. They already know how to eat off forks."

"Bud Shumway, if your mother could see you..."

"I learned it from my dad," Bud grinned.

His mom had been a stickler for good manners, and she frowned on feeding dogs under the table, though his dad had always slipped food to their old dog, Rascal.

Wilma Jean sighed. "I have a really busy day tomorrow. Vern and I are supplying a group going out by Factory Butte."

"Can't they just drive in there?" Bud asked.

"They can, but then they can't. They're going way out on foot, and we're going to drop their camping gear and supplies."

"What are they doing?"

"It's some kind of photography group. They're going to be out there for several weeks."

Bud replied, "I would love to spend a few weeks out like that."

"It would be good for you. You need a break. We really need to slow down, hon. We're both too busy. We've been here before, remember?"

Bud recalled how he'd gotten so burned out as sheriff that he'd actually resigned at one point, Howie taking over. He now thought of Shorty's farm, and even though he figured it probably wasn't the best time to mention it, he told Wilma Jean all about Shorty's proposal.

"It seems like we're getting busier and busier," she replied. "But hon, I really need some time to think about it. Tell Shorty I'm interested, assuming you want to do the fields, but I need to figure out the logistics."

She paused, then continued. "I think business is just going to keep booming. More and more people are discovering the canyons. People come out here away from the hustle and bustle of their lives and find that being out away from all their problems is therapeutic."

Bud said, "I agree. They come out here for the adventure, thinking they're just going to have a good time, then they discover what it's like to sit around a campfire under a big canyon wall, far from the daily news and grind. Then they don't want to go back."

Wilma Jean said, "Right. You know, hon, we're very lucky to live out here where we can enjoy the peace and quiet any time we want. You just take a little drive, and there you are, nobody for miles, though that's going to change if people keep coming."

Bud was now cleaning the dishes off the table, giving the dogs the last few scraps. He replied, "Maybe we should take Shorty up on his offer. I think we're going to see more tourists, and another B&B might be a good thing."

Wilma Jean replied, "Well, we'd definitely have to hire someone to run it. Molly's got her hands full over at the Melon View. Actually, maybe this area could use more lodging. I really haven't had time to think about it, but if we're so busy over at the Melon View, it means there's a demand. But who could we get to run it?"

Bud answered, "It's so nice, we'd want someone with a bit of flair who could make it a great experience. And it has a small apartment in the back, so a manager could stay there."

Wilma Jean now handed Bud a cup of hot chocolate, saying, "Let's think about it. But there's a full moon tonight. Let's take the dogs out and sit on the porch and enjoy it for once. Bring your harmonica."

Bud was surprised but pleased, and he followed his wife outside into the cool evening, the dogs at their heels, taking his harmonica from his pocket.

"Play that song you wrote when you were up in the Yukon, hon, the one when you were way out in the middle of nowhere all alone. You know, the one you call *The Yukon Trail*."

Bud began softy playing, and it quickly took him back to when he was wandering, all alone, out in some of the wildest most remote country he'd ever seen. It was also some of the most beautiful, with its feeling of distance and solitude.

After playing for awhile, he put his harmonica down and began softly singing the lyrics he'd been working on.

> Northern stars hang in the sky,
> Wind calls through the lonesome pines,
> All the world is like a dream,
> And how bright the moon can seem,
> On the Yukon Trail.
>
> Nights are cold and winter's long,
> But a new world's born each dawn,
> Howling wolves call far away,

Sunrise brings a brand new day,
On the Yukon Trail.

Northern Lights bring memories,
Your sweet voice calls out to me,
Scarlet fireweed, sky so blue,
Happy times, a heart so true,
On the Yukon Trail.

His wife sighed, and as the dogs curled up at their feet, Bud thought back to how alone he'd felt way up north, and how glad he was to be back home.

Putting his arm around Wilma Jean's shoulders, he knew that whatever they decided, it would all work out just fine.

---

## 20

"Careful, if you make Jasper mad enough, he might just bite himself."

A tall lanky man laughed at his own joke as his companion, a short stocky fellow, grimaced.

"I'm more likely to bite *you*, Leon," the shorter man growled, then turned to where Bud and Shorty stood. "I just wanna know hows come you lawmen think it's OK to barge in here like you own the place."

Bud and Shorty stood in front of an old dugout near the Cactus Rat Mine where a hand-painted sign nailed above the doorjamb read, "Yellow Cat Cafe, Welcome."

They'd come in Bud's sheriff's vehicle, a green Land Cruiser with the emblem of the Emery County Sheriff on each door, Lindie waiting on the back seat. An old rusted army ambulance sat nearby with license plates that Bud noted were from 1958.

The tall fellow named Leon had blonde hair that came down to his shoulders, and Bud couldn't decide if it was naturally curly or just so tangled it looked that way. Nor could he tell if the guy's counterpart, who he'd called Jasper, even had hair, for he was wearing a yellow baseball cap pulled down over his ears, its insignia so faded it was illegible.

Bud didn't know if the two men were partly made out of sand or just hadn't bathed for years. The short stocky man wore old tan mechanic's coveralls with, of all things, faded army-green gators that came up almost to his knees, the tops tied snug with strings and the words 10th Mountain Division stamped on them in faded white.

The blonde-haired man wore torn jeans and a striped golf-style nylon shirt that looked like something the Bucket of Bolts Overlanders would condone, as well as a silver chain around his neck, which to Bud looked incongruous way out in the Big Empty. Both had scuffed boots that looked like the soles were about to fall off.

Now the fellow called Leon was saying with disdain, "What hospitality! And what a memory! You invited them here, Jasper. You dictated the letter to me, remember?"

"How could they get it that fast?" Jasper answered, then turned to Bud. "So, you're Sheriff Shumway? Man, you're a lot more responsive than that Radium sheriff, I'll grant you that."

"That's probably a good thing," Leon smiled. "'Cause if Sheriff Stocks came out here very often, we'd be history. But come on inside, boys, and we'll make you some coffee, unless you forgot to bring some along."

Bud grinned. He reached through the back window of the Land Cruiser and pulled out a paper sack, handing it to Leon. It held a pound of Wicked Brew coffee, two packages of Kebler Goldfish Crackers, a large box of matches, and a half-dozen bottles of Old Man Green's watermelon spritzer, as well as two barbecue beef sandwiches from Howie's Drive-In.

He and Shorty had stopped at Howie's on their way out of town and stocked up on lunch for themselves, then decided to get extra in case they made it to the Yellow Cat Cafe.

"It's kind of unusual to have to bring food to the proprietors of a cafe," Shorty said. "What do you serve here, anyway?"

"C'mon inside," Jasper said, ignoring Shorty. "Watch your head."

The dugout was dark inside, as was to be expected, thought Bud, but once his eyes were used to it, he noted how tidy and clean everything was.

Cots sat in two corners, each with bright red Marmot sleeping bags, and a HAM radio outfit sat on an old crate in another corner, wires running outside to what Bud assumed was a generator. Next to an old folding metal table with a two-burner Coleman stove sat a banjo, and near that an expensive Yeti cooler, behind which was an assortment of camping gear that included several high-tech folding camp chairs, a Clam screen tent still in its bag, a small Dutch oven, and a box full of freeze-dried dinners with labels like *Beef Stew*, *Chicken Teriyaki*, and *Blueberry Pancakes*. Next to the HAM outfit was an expensive-looking red porcelain mug with the words, *Rainier Park Blanket, Pendleton Woolen Mills*.

"Anyway, to answer your question, Mr.—I don't believe we've been introduced," Jasper said, looking at Shorty.

"Shorty Doyle," Shorty said.

"I'm Leon, and this is Jasper," Leon said.

They all shook hands as Jasper finished his thought.

"We serve whatever you bring with you, that's how it works. But one thing you'll find different here is that we don't charge you a dime. Not even a penny. And you don't have to tip. We're very unique that way. But is barbecue on today's menu? I smell something good."

Leon pulled out the sandwiches, handing Jasper one, who grinned.

"Man oh man, you fellows can come eat here any time you want," he said. "Put the coffeepot on, Leon."

Leon poured water from a small jug into a percolator pot that Bud figured was probably from the original uranium boom days, then dumped in some Wicked Brew and set it on the burner. He then pulled out two camp chairs and handed Bud and Shorty each one.

Bud now thought of Cal and the missing gear from the campers at the park and said, "These are really nice chairs. Very lightweight. Where'd you get them?"

Jasper replied, "We won them in a *Reader's Digest* contest. We enter lots of magazine contests and are pretty lucky. Got all this stuff that way."

Bud nodded his head as Shorty raised his eyebrows, looking

skeptical.

Leon, noting Shorty's look, added, "People bring us magazines and we enter all the contests. Sometimes cereal boxes have them, too. We put the entries in our mailbox. By the way, did you get our letter there or did someone bring it to you?"

"I was out there the other day and saw the flag was up, so I stopped. That's a pretty ingenious system you have," Bud said.

"Thanks, it was my idea," Jasper replied.

"No, I came up with it," Leon argued.

"Well, I'm the one who got the mailbox," Jasper said testily. "Not so easy getting mailboxes out here."

Bud recalled the Desert Star address on it, marked out.

"You boys live out here?" Shorty asked.

"We do, and we're perfectly legal," Jasper answered.

The topic had obviously come up before, Bud noted, as Leon now handed him and Shorty each a mug of hot coffee, one with the words *Poison Spider Cycling* and the other reading *Chico Hot Springs*.

Noting Bud's interest, Leon said, "People come by and leave us mugs all the time. They like our coffee, I guess."

"How are you legal?" Shorty persisted. "Isn't this BLM land? Just curious."

Jasper, looking irritated, said, "This is a state land section. We have a claim, legal as that fancy gold-nugget belt buckle you're wearing. We can renew it every five years as long as we're workin' it."

Bud, surprised, asked, "Uranium?"

"Now who in their right mind would prospect for uranium these days?" Jasper shook his head. "Ain't worth a dime. No, we have a meteorite claim."

Shorty snorted, "A meteorite claim? How in hellsbells can you have a meteorite claim? Nobody knows where a meteor is going to fall."

"We're aware of that, but apparently the folks at the State Lands headquarters aren't," Jasper grinned.

"But how do you work a claim like that?" Bud asked.

"Easy," Leon replied. "You just walk around every so often with a magnet, looking to see if anything new fell. You know, most meteorites are about 10 percent iron."

"Do you find a lot of meteorites?" Shorty asked. "They can be worth quite a bit, you know."

Leon replied, "We found one out in the Burr Desert over by Hanksville once. Seen a few come down, but couldn't find them. But say, where did you get that gold nugget, anyway? Not around here, I would guess."

Shorty laughed, then said, "I found it in the Yukon. But what's this on your gators, Jasper? Were you in the 10th Mountain Division at one time?"

Jasper looked surprised, but pleased. "You know what that is?"

"I do. My dad was in it."

"No kidding? I have my old skis out back. Wanna see them?"

Jasper and Shorty left the dugout, and Bud asked Leon, "10th Mountain Division? That's World War II stuff. Jasper's a lot older than he looks, eh?"

Leon replied, "Let's just say that he has enough years under his belt to have perfected the art of lying."

Now Bud said, "Say, Leon, we listened to your broadcast the other evening, well, anyway, I listened to a recording of it. Was that fellow who sang the Willy Nelson tunes named Jay by any chance? If so, do you have any idea where he's at?"

"Yes, his name was Jay. Is he in some kind of trouble?"

"Not at all. We came out here some time ago and got him unstuck, and I'm just wondering what became of him."

"Well, after he got stuck he got smart and went into Radium and rented a Jeep from Cliff-Wrangler and got himself outfitted up, then came back out here. That's when he agreed to sing on the show. But he's gone, now."

"Do you know where he went?" Bud asked.

"He said he was looking for the woman in the little red car. You know, the one we mentioned in our letter? She probably got stuck, too—or was abducted by a UFO."

Bud was confused, for it had now been awhile since they'd found

Marie's body. Jay obviously didn't know she was dead if he was still looking for her.

"How long ago was he here?"

"He left this morning. Camped out by the mine last night. Drove us crazy out there singing. Jasper finally shot off his rifle so he'd stop. He said he was headed for Winter Camp territory—you know, that upland back over to the east. Left us a nice box of fudge, said it would melt before he could eat it. I'd offer you a piece, but cafes don't usually serve fudge, so we ate it all."

"Did he say why he was going over to Winter Camp?"

"He didn't, but we assumed he was going after that woman. He said he was worried about her getting lost. We saw Kelso out here not long after, and if they meet up with him, they'll get lost for sure—Kelso gets everyone lost, including himself. I'm surprised he was even out here, 'cause he does most of his exploring on Google Earth anymore—whatever Google Earth is—at least, that's what he told Jasper. Said it was some kind of satellite thing. Really upset Jasper to think he might be being spied on like that. I didn't have the heart to tell him there's more out there watchin' him than just some satellite."

Bud was now even more confused.

"Who's Kelso?"

"He writes guidebooks."

Bud now thought back to the fellow at the cafe counter, then asked, "And when did you last see the woman?"

"Oh, she had her little red sportster out here yesterday, and I know she has to be stuck by now, but hopefully Jay will find her. I couldn't believe she even got it out this far."

"And she was sort of small, dark haired, dressed in black, with New York plates?"

"That's her. Is she in some kind of trouble?"

Bud replied, "Not that I know of, unless ghosts can get into trouble."

Shorty was now back, ready to go, and they said their goodbyes, leaving Leon scratching his head in puzzlement, or at least the part he could get to through the sand and thick curls.

## 21

Bud and Shorty had stopped down the road a ways from the Yellow Cat Cafe, where Bud waited in the Land Cruiser with Lindie while Shorty hid up in the rocks.

Bud now got out of the vehicle with Lindie, then let her sniff Shorty's straw hat, saying, "Get 'em, Lindie. Get Shorty!"

Lindie jumped up excitedly, trying to grab the hat, then began running around Bud in circles. The more he encouraged her, the more excited she got, now barking.

Bud wasn't sure how to even begin training a SAR dog, but this didn't seem to be working. He again let her sniff Shorty's hat, but she managed to grab it from him and began playing keep-away as Bud tried to retrieve it.

Now Shorty, watching from behind the rocks and seeing his hat was in danger, yelled at Lindie, who immediately ran to him with the hat. Shorty, now laughing, came back from the rocks, Lindie at his side.

Bud groaned. He was pretty sure this wasn't how a search-and-rescue training session was supposed to go.

"I think I need to study up on this a bit," Bud said, getting two watermelon spritzers from the Land Cruiser. He could now see a rooster-tail of dust coming down the road. "Sure is busy out here," he commented. "This will be the third vehicle we've seen out here today."

"It's all those rock hounds," Shorty replied. "I was kind of surprised at how many were at my lecture. Seems like word's getting out more each year about the rock show."

"Agreed," Bud said as a dusty SUV went by, its occupants waving.

Handing Shorty a spritzer, Bud said, "You think that Jasper fellow was really in the 10th Mountain Division?"

"Nah," Shorty replied. "All he had was an old pair of rental skis with *Property of Ski Sunlight* stickers. You know, I learned a lot about the 10th from my dad. They were a light infantry division specially trained for mountain fighting and were based over in Colorado at Camp Hale. They skied into the Austrian Alps during World War II and defeated the Germans there. But that's not why Jasper took me back there, he said he wanted to get away from Leon so he could talk in private. He told me he's worried about what's going on out there."

"Just like in his letter, eh?" Bud said. "I wondered why he never mentioned it, since it was supposedly why he wanted us to come out. But did he say why he was worried? Why keep it from Leon, since he was the one who wrote the letter?"

"He said Leon's way out in left field, and he doesn't want to talk to him about it anymore."

"Talk about what?" Bud asked.

"Well, he wasn't sure himself, but he wanted me to tell you that somebody out here in the Yellow Cat is doing something illegal. I told him I thought that was kind of ironic, coming from a guy who's apparently outfitting himself from the tourists over in the park. He didn't deny it, but said that at least his activities were honorable because he was just trying to survive."

Bud shook his head. "You need high-tech camp chairs and expensive Marmot bags to survive? But did he have any clues as to what's going on?"

"Well," Shorty replied, watching as a Toyota 4Runner drove by, "He said that this guide-book author Kelso was up to no good."

"Up to no good?" Bud asked. "Did he say what kind of no good?"

"He said they keep having people come to the cafe saying their vehicles have disappeared and they need a ride out."

"Vehicles disappeared? Way out here? Who in hellsbells would steal a vehicle out here, and where would a thief take it?"

Bud thought back to how he'd reassured Jay his vehicle had been in no danger sitting there with the keys in it.

"Jasper said Leon thinks aliens are involved, though he can't ever come up with any details as to why they'd want to steal people's vehicles. That's why he doesn't want to talk to him about it any more. But Bud, if something like that is going on, it would be criminal to leave people stranded out here with no food or water. A person could easily die before they were found, especially since most of this country has no cell phone service."

"Granted," Bud replied. "Did he say how often this was happening? A lot of people or just one or two?"

"I didn't ask," Shorty replied. "At that point, he acted like he was done talking about it. He was trying to get me to go check out his can dump, but I begged off and came back inside."

"Why would Leon think aliens were involved?" Bud asked.

"Well, Jasper told me a story, and I'm guessing it's just another of his tall tales, but maybe Hum could verify it if you asked. Supposedly, it was night time and some guy was driving along Highway 6—this was before the freeway was built—and he looked up to see a big light coming down on him from up on the Bookcliffs. Jasper says it was in the newspaper, and he didn't just make it all up."

"He must be aware of his reputation," Bud remarked.

"Well, next thing this guy knew, he was being picked up off the highway by a State Trooper who'd seen him lying there. He had no memory of anything after seeing the light. His pickup was gone, and a search turned up nothing. They thought maybe he'd driven it off the road and wrecked and had a head injury, but they couldn't find the truck. So, this trooper took the fellow to the hospital in Radium, and when he went in the next day to see how he was and ask a few more questions, the fellow was gone. The night nurse said some military guys had come in the middle of the night and taken him away. And that's the last they heard of him."

"And this was supposedly in the paper? When was all this?" Bud asked.

"He didn't say, and it sure has the ring of a conspiracy theory to me. But there's more."

Shorty continued. "Sometime later, someone was flying across the Books and saw a pickup way up in the cliffs—we're talking several thousand feet up high in a place no one could ever drive to. Apparently the sheriff at the time, probably Buckshot Williams, flew up there and saw it with his own two eyes. But the funny thing is, a couple of weeks later it was gone, and people in Thompson Springs reported seeing military choppers in the area."

"Sounds pretty far-fetched," Bud replied. "But I'll ask Hum next time I talk to him."

Shorty now nodded as another vehicle came up the road. "This looks like somebody pulling something."

Just then, Tex Tanner's yellow Jeep Cherokee drove by, the words *Tanner Towing and Off-Road Recovery* on the side. He was towing another vehicle, which just happened to be a small red roadster. As it went by, Bud could see the plates were from New York and read, "IWRITE."

Bud was shocked. It had been two days now since Marie's body had been found, and Hum had said Tex was recovering the vehicle. The car had already been gone when he'd examined Marie's tracks. Had Tex taken it somewhere else and was only now taking it back to Radium? If so, why?

It just didn't make sense, as well as the fact that Jasper and Leon had reported the car being at the Yellow Cat Cafe just the previous day—with a woman driver who fit Marie's description.

"Jump in," Bud said. "I need to find out what's going on."

With that, he and Shorty were soon hot on Tex's tail, though it was hard to make him out through the cloud of dust. Bud turned on his lights, then eventually his siren, but Tex just kept going.

Finally tired of eating dust, Bud pulled over.

"I don't think he even knows we're back here," he told Shorty. "I'll call Hum later and find out what's going on."

Shorty shrugged as Bud added, "Let's go on home."

## 22

It was late evening by the time they got back, and Bud dropped Shorty off at the Westwind, where he'd left his truck, then drove on into downtown Green River.

He noticed right away that something was different, but he couldn't quite put his finger on it. It finally dawned on him that the bright neon lights of Howie's Drive-In were off, as well as the interior lights, and a big *Closed* sign stood in the front window. And just down the block, the Melon Rind Cafe also looked deserted, its outside lights off.

Bud pulled over in front of the Melon Rind, parking next to Maureen's green VW Bug, and got out. The cafe door wasn't locked, and as he went inside, he could see it was empty, Maureen nowhere around.

He went into the kitchen looking for her, wondering if everything was alright. To his surprise, there stood Howie, white as a sheet, wringing his hands as Maureen leaned against the wall.

"I don't know what to do, Sheriff," Howie said. "She's going to have the baby. I don't know what to do."

Bud answered, "It's OK, Howie, we'll get her to the hospital. You guys go sit down while I try to get Wilma Jean on the phone."

Howie helped Maureen into the cafe's dining area, where she began pacing back and forth as Bud dialed Wilma Jean.

Wilma Jean answered, "Hon, I just got back, and if you can get her to the airstrip on the farm, I'll fly her to the hospital in Radium."

"We'll meet you there in about ten minutes," Bud told her.

Now Maureen was sitting in the booth as Howie paced back and forth.

"Howie, we're going to take Maureen to the farm's airstrip. Are you ready to go? Does she have an overnight bag packed?"

Howie nodded, then ran to the VW, grabbing a small bag from the car. He then said nervously, "Sheriff, I don't think I can do this by myself."

Bud replied, "Howie, you and Wilma Jean can fly Maureen to Radium. It's lots quicker than driving. I'll call ahead and have an ambulance sent out to pick you guys up at the airport to take you to the hospital. I think you have plenty of time."

Howie stood looking at Bud, then said, "I'm not sure what to do, Bud. Can't you go with us?"

"Howie, someone needs to stay here and take care of things. We can't have us both gone in case there's an emergency. But it'll be OK, Deputy. Wilma Jean's invaluable and can coach you if Maureen starts having the baby."

"I *am* a deputy, aren't I?" Howie said, looking relieved. He then pulled his set of keys from his pocket, ran outside, and jumped into the Land Cruiser, turning on the siren and starting to back out as Lindie quickly jumped from the front into the back seat.

Bud shook his head as Maureen gathered herself enough to start laughing. He turned to her, saying, "I'm pretty sure Wilma Jean's going to want to stay down in Radium with you guys until the baby's born. I think Howie's going to need the moral support."

Maureen smiled. "Probably more than *I* will, I would guess."

Bud shook his head. "Howie may end up in the hospital himself if his nerves don't calm down."

Howie was soon back inside looking sheepish, and he and Bud helped Maureen through the cafe door and into the Land Cruiser.

As Bud locked up the cafe, he noticed that someone had written on the chalkboard: "Today's Special: Little Malcolm McPherson."

Now on their way, Bud called the Radium County EMT office for an ambulance, Howie and Maureen in the back seat, her head on his shoulder, Lindie having jumped back into the front.

They were soon at the strip Vern had bulldozed along one of the farm fields, where Wilma Jean waited for them by her pink Cessna. Howie and Maureen got into the plane, and Wilma Jean eased it down the strip, quickly taking to the sky.

It wasn't like her to dawdle in such circumstances, Bud thought, proud of her flying skills, thinking it hadn't really been that long ago that he'd worried about her becoming a pilot. She seemed like an old pro now, and he was glad she'd learned so quickly.

As the plane's drone faded into the twilight, Bud let Lindie out for a moment. He'd go home and get Hoppie and Pierre, then go over to Howie's and make sure the cats were fed and put Little Bun into her cage for the night. He'd then bring the dogs back over to the farm for a few minutes before it got dark, as he was feeling he'd been neglecting them lately for Lindie.

He could smell the rich loam of freshly plowed fields, and he looked over to Shorty's farm, where he could see lights on in Shorty's house. It gave him a pastoral homey feel, and he again felt that poignancy that often followed him around, a mixture of gratitude for the security of his home mixed with the call of the wild. Here, in Green River, he was lucky to have the farm and their bungalow and yet be able to get out into wild country at the drop of the hat.

Bud now climbed into the Land Cruiser, Lindie by his side, figuring that by the time he got back home that evening, the baby boy who Maureen had already named Malcolm would be celebrating his very own birthday.

Bud wondered if he'd take after Howie with his love of science and astronomy or be more like his mom, with her love of animals and cooking. Since both loved music, he suspected the little guy would be musical, and he hoped Malcolm would have a long happy life, even though he was pretty sure he hadn't been born yet.

As he pulled onto Long Street, heading toward the bungalow, he caught the scent of a flowering crabapple tree wafting from someone's yard. For some reason, it made him think of Marie Lee, whose life had been sadly cut short.

He vowed to get back on the case that evening after dinner, for he knew Wilma Jean wouldn't be coming home. He'd be on his own, wanting something to distract him from how lonely the bungalow could sometimes feel without her.

## 23

Bud leaned back in his recliner, the dogs sleeping at his feet, everyone happily full of leftover stew. He'd taken them for a nice walk on the farm, and while at Howie's, had noticed *The Last Opera Show* on his desk and decided to take Howie up on his offer and borrow it. He once again thought it might just hold some kind of clue as to why its author was now dead.

He opened it to where Howie's bookmark divided the pages and began reading.

> I watched her face closely as I said, "Here's some good news. Your father isn't turning into a werewolf."
>
> Her eyes opened wide.
>
> "He's not crazy, either," I added. "Even though he sings opera."
>
> She was gobsmacked. "But...then..."
>
> "What's wrong with him? He's ill, Miss Thaddeus. He has a very rare disease known as porphyria. I'm almost positive. Has all the symptoms. It's just a matter of getting him to a doctor for treatment."
>
> "It can be treated?" She looked like she was in a daze.
>
> "I'll give you the number of a physician who's an authority on the disease. You and your father can take it from there."

*She now put her hands over her face and burst into tears.*

*I said, "Things are going to be alright. It's made him act quite different, I know, but now you know why. That and the locoweed."*

*Now I could see the headlights of what appeared to be a truck coming down the highway.*

*"You have to go now," she said. "It's my ex-husband, Nails. Hurry."*

*As she ducked away into the darkness, I heard the tiny metal purr of an expensive engine starting, and then a Shelby Cobra came out of the garage door, Nails behind the wheel. The red paint on it was so new it shimmered. I watched as $100,000 worth of wheels went up the ramp and into the dark belly of the truck trailer. Nails reappeared in the door of the trailer, jumped to the ground, and went back into the garage.*

Bud stopped. Nails was her ex? Had he just painted a stolen car? And this was the second mention of locoweed he'd seen in the book. Was it some kind of clue?

Marie had a sketch of locoweed, and she'd even apparently dug some up and even ground the calyx into powder. Locoweed was a fairly common plant, but why did she keep mentioning it?

He pulled out his harmonica and began playing, then abruptly stopped and turned on his computer. It was time to do the research he'd been putting off, not really knowing where to start.

He wondered what porphyria was, the disease mentioned in the book. He keyed in the word and read:

**Porphyria**

*Noun: a rare hereditary disease in which the blood pigment hemoglobin is abnormally metabolized. Symptoms include mental disturbances and extreme sensitivity of the skin to light, which leads victims to avoid daylight, hence its historical reference as the vampire disease. There is no known cure.*

Interesting, he thought, but not really much of a clue. He now looked up the definition of locoweed.

*Locoweed*

*Noun: a widely distributed plant of the pea family that, if eaten by livestock, can cause a brain disorder, the symptoms of which include unpredictable behavior and loss of coordination. Also called vetch. Genus Astragalus, family Leguminosae.*

Bud found it odd that both porphyria and locoweed had similar symptoms: mental disturbances and unpredictable behavior. One was apparently a genetic disease, since it was hereditary, while the other was the result of ingesting the plant.

He now dug deeper.

*Locoweed is a common perennial plant found throughout the western United States. Its seeds can lie dormant for 50 years. Its flowers look similar to sweet pea flowers, and can be blue, purple, yellow, or white. There are more than 300 species of locoweed, most of which are toxic.*

*Locoweed gets its name from the Spanish word loco (crazy) from the abnormal behavior of poisoned animals, which results from neurologic damage. Locoweed can also cause congestive heart failure. There is no effective treatment for locoweed poisoning.*

*The disease is chronic, developing after weeks of ingesting locoweed, and begins with depression, dull-appearing eyes, and incoordination, progressing to uncharacteristic behavior including aggression, staggering, and solitary behavior, along with wasting, and ending in death if continued consumption is allowed. Vision may also be affected.*

*Swainsonine is the toxic alkaloid found in locoweed. An animal suspected of locoweed poisoning must have its blood sampled within two days of eating locoweed for there to be detectable levels of swainsonine.*

*Some locoweed species also accumulate selenium. This has led to confusion between swainsonine poisoning and selenium poisoning due to this genus.*

*Some studies suggest that swainsonine may have a useful application in fighting cancer. It also has immunostimulating activity.*

Bud sat back, his coffee now cold. Had Marie been a victim of locoweed poisoning? Had it been ongoing, or had she simply ingested enough there under the juniper tree to actually kill her? Had she done it to herself?

Maybe she was trying to cure herself from some disease, Bud thought, though it seemed like a case where the cure could be worse than the disease. Did she have porphyria?

He now remembered Howie asking him what Marie's sister's name was. He wasn't sure where to start, so he searched on *Marie Lee*. It was a fairly common name and brought up too many hits, so he tried narrowing it down to *Marie Lee author*.

The search brought up the *New York Times* article about plagiarism, as well as similar articles in other papers, but nothing really new. He clicked on an article in the *Washington Post*, and there it was! Bingo! A photo, not just of Marie, but of her sister.

The two were standing next to each other, smiling. They almost looked like twins, small and dark haired, though Marie was somewhat slighter and had an air about her of defeat, while her sister seemed more self-confident. Bud wasn't sure how he got that impression, but it seemed to be from the expressions on their faces.

The caption read: *Marie Lee and her younger sister Rosalind Lee in better days. Rosalind has vowed to wear only black until a cure is found.*

Bud wondered what was going on that they would refer to the past as better days, but the rest of the article was behind a paywall, requiring a subscription. He wondered if both sisters hadn't just found out they had something wrong. Was it porphyria?

He at least now knew for sure that Marie's sister was Rosalind Lee, and maybe he could find out more by doing a search on her. She was supposedly a famous mystery writer, after all, so he should find plenty of material. But since it was getting late and he was tired, he decided to get back on it the next day.

It was then that it dawned on him that perhaps he'd missed the boat and maybe wasn't much of a detective after all, for he suddenly realized that Rosalind Lee was at that very moment not 2,000 miles away in New York City, but possibly right here, out in the nearby Yellow Cat.

She was the one who'd come into the cafe, not Marie. And now her car had just been towed by Tex Tanner, leaving her stranded out in the wilds, just like all the others Jasper and Leon had mentioned whose vehicles Tanner had taken.

## 24

Bud sat out on the back patio, looking at the stars. After shutting down the computer, he'd grabbed several biscuits for the dogs, then got himself a small bowl of vanilla-bean ice cream. After all, Wilma Jean was gone, so he might as well cut loose a little.

The dogs happily crunching their biscuits, he thought of Marie Lee, then of her sister Rosalind, who he suspected was somewhere out in the Yellow Cat. Did she have any kind of survival gear, or even a warm coat? Based on how she'd been dressed when she'd come into the cafe, he figured she was woefully unprepared for much of anything, yet alone a night out in the desert. And even though it was spring, the nights were still cold.

But something felt off. Hadn't Maureen said she recognized the woman in the cafe from the picture on the back cover of *The Last Opera Show*? Bud hadn't seen the woman's face, but Maureen had, and she'd said it was the author, who would be Marie. But Hum had said Marie was dead.

Whoever it was, Bud wondered if he shouldn't be going back out to look for her. He knew Jay had rented a Jeep—maybe she was with him and both were fine. And what exactly had they been doing out there in the first place?

Bud decided he should call Shorty and see if he wanted to go back out tomorrow, but it was getting late. He'd get a good night's sleep, then give Shorty a call in the morning, and maybe the two of them could go out and see what they could find. The woman had to be Rosalind, and maybe she and Jay were both back at the Yellow Cat Cafe by now.

Ice cream now finished, Bud was starting to get chilly, so he took the dogs back inside. Putting his dishes in the dishwasher, he wondered how things were going down in Radium and if little Malcolm had been born yet.

He wasn't surprised to hear his phone ring, thinking it was probably Wilma Jean with a progress report. He was surprised, however, to see the caller ID read Radium County Sheriff.

Was something wrong? Had something bad happened? He always worried when his wife took off in a plane, though he was getting much better about it.

"Yell-ow," he answered, half holding his breath.

"Bud, this is Hum. Sorry to bother you so late. We're having a minor crisis here in Radium. The Colorado's running 30,000 cfs and a big old cottonwood came down and wrapped itself around one of the bridge abutments, and we've had to shut down the highway into town. That's an old bridge, and we're taking no chances, as debris is collecting around it. And before you ask, yes, your wife and everyone made it in before it happened. They're at the hospital, but I don't know anything about the baby. But I wanted you to know nobody's coming in or out of Radium until this is resolved, and it may be a day or two."

Bud sighed, then asked, "What about the River Road?"

"It's closed, too. We have some places where it's undercut and unsafe. The only way out of here is to go clear around through Colorado and the Paradox Valley, or by chopper. Can't even get to the airport."

"Well, thanks for letting me know. I've been meaning to call you anyway about the Marie Lee case. Hum, I have a couple of quick questions. Are you sure Tex Tanner recovered Marie Lee's car the same day you found her?"

Hum paused, then said, "I'm sure, Bud. It's in our impound lot right now."

"A little red roadster with New York plates?"

"One and the same. What's going on?"

"Do you know what the plates read?" Bud asked.

"Sure, they're easy to remember—they're vanity plates. IPAINT."

"IPAINT?" Bud asked, surprised.

"Yeah, the woman must've been a painter."

"I thought she was a writer," Bud commented. "But Hum, I saw Tanner hauling one just like it out of the Yellow Cat today. I think it must be her sister's. New York plates with IWRITE."

"Well, that's odd," Hum replied. "I didn't even know she had a sister. And driving the same kind of car? Maybe they were twins or something."

"I don't think they were," Bud replied. "Though they looked very similar. Hum, keep an eye out for that car. I think Tanner's up to something. But one more question, then I'll let you go. Do you know anything about a fellow whose pickup was found way up in the Books after he disappeared from the hospital? Ever hear that story?"

Hum laughed. "That's been making the rounds since the days of Buckshot Williams. Nothing to it, just a wild story. No verification of any kind. But Bud, I gotta run. I'll be in touch."

As Bud hung up, he knew he'd be on his own for awhile, and he suddenly felt abandoned. He could easily take care of Howie and Maureen's critters, as well as his and Wilma Jean's affairs, except for one thing—no, two things—the Melon Rind and Howie's Drive-In would both be out of commission for awhile, as would Wilma Jean's home-cooked meals. But he'd already known that, and the bridge being closed really didn't affect him yet, except he couldn't go to Radium, but he hadn't been planning to anyway.

He now got ready for bed, feeling out of sorts, knowing Wilma Jean, Howie, and Maureen were close, yet far away. He wished his wife would call.

He then thought of Shorty and Cassie out on Cassie's ranch and felt a sense of relief. He knew he could depend on them, no matter what might come his way, and they might even feed him a nice meal or two, if he could just get up the courage to ask.

He slipped into bed and was soon fast asleep, all three dogs curled up next to him. He was soon dreaming about *The Last Opera Show*, but instead of reading the book, he was somehow now the detective *in* the book.

---

## 25

*It started to drizzle.*

*I swiveled my chair around to look out my office window to the wharf. An oil tanker was there. So was a barge. A giant reptilian crane was unloading cargo containers, its monstrous hand swinging back and forth.*

*I could see my name, in reverse, printed on the outside of the glass door, raindrops starting to make it blurry: Bud Shumway, Private Investigator.*

*OK. That explained everything, including why I was talking to myself like this.*

*The sky got darker. Rain fell. I'd stopped earlier at a deli, picking up a pastrami and Swiss on rye for lunch. I laid it to one side and turned on my answering machine. Someone had called over and over again without leaving a message.*

*I picked up the phone and dialed Sergeant Howie O'Pherson. The big-city Irish cop had worked me into a situation I didn't understand. I knew the sergeant was just trying to do his job, but either everyone was crazy, or everyone was lying. It didn't matter which right then. I wanted to get to the bottom of things. Actually, I wanted to get out of town, but I was broke.*

*Sergeant Howie didn't answer. I knew he was avoiding me. I now badly wanted a dollop of vanilla-bean ice cream, but my fridge was empty. I couldn't help myself, though I knew it wouldn't go with the rotgut whisky I was drinking. Don't ask how I knew.*

*Just then, I saw something through the bullet-riddled glass of my office door. A bright-pink stretch Masarati had just pulled up in the rain. A uniformed driver opened the side door and a woman got out, then came inside without knocking.*

*She was wearing a slinky black dress and a black pill-box hat with a pink feather in the brim and carried a pink ostrich-skin purse. She smiled as she sat down, even though she was drenched. I could smell something sweet. It reminded me of apple pie. I knew right away she was trouble.*

*"I'm the Widow Wilma Jean," she said, her voice dripping with honey.*

*She was beautiful, and I could tell she knew it.*

*"What happened to your husband?" I asked warily.*

*"He bought the farm," she replied, taking a red lipstick from her purse and patting it on her lips.*

*I flinched. Things didn't feel right. I needed something to fiddle with. I looked around for my Smith and Wesson, but it was somehow missing.*

*She put the lipstick away. I thought I saw a glint of pink metal as she closed her purse.*

*"I want the book, and I'm willing to pay for it," she said.*

*"What book?" I asked innocently.*

*I was now desperate for something to fiddle with. I spied my holster on the floor. That darn wiener dog I'd won betting at the dog tracks was chewing on it again. They'd told me his name was Pierre, but right then, it was Mud.*

*I picked up my gun and took out a Magnum .357 bullet as the Widow Wilma Jean watched. I began fiddling with it.*

*"What book?" The Widow Wilma Jean repeated my question mockingly. She then whispered, "The book you tried to kill Pawnshop Goldie for."*

*"I didn't try to kill Pawnshop Goldie. Somebody wanted to make it look that way," I said tersely. "I've never set foot in his pawn shop."*

*"If you didn't try to kill him, who did?" The Widow Wilma Jean asked with suspicion. "Someone wants him dead."*

*I was getting frustrated. "Good question. If you're looking for a killer, sweetheart, you've got the wrong guy."*

"OK, suppose I believe you." She tossed her head as her voice went back to sweet.

I replied, "Suppose you tell me about the book."

"It's a diary."

I was confused. A diary? Nobody wrote diaries any more, they wrote journals.

"Whose diary?" I asked.

"My friend Rosie's."

"I don't know anyone named Rosie," I replied.

The Widow Wilma Jean now looked angry.

"Whoever stole Rosie's diary messed it all up with locoweed recipes. They also stole her snake. They want Goldie dead."

I fiddled with the bullet. The wiener dog chewed on my pant leg. It continued to rain.

The Widow Wilma Jean now stood and opened her pink ostrich-skin purse, taking out a small pouch and placing it on my desk.

"There's more where this came from," she said, then walked to the door. She turned, saying, "And don't forget, the punishment should fit the crime."

With that, she walked out.

The rain came down even harder.

I carefully opened the pouch. It held a business card with an elegant script that read, "The Widow Wilma Jean" along with her number. It also held a blood-red lipstick.

I knew beyond all doubt that she was trying to run some kind of confidence game on me, and I knew I wasn't about to fall for it. I had no use for a lipstick, and she knew it.

But the package held something else, something far more insidious.

Wrapped in thick wax paper was something soft and warm. I slowly unwrapped it. My suspicions were confirmed—it was a piece of fresh-baked homemade apple pie.

I took in the aroma. It was something I hadn't smelled for a long time. It made me homesick for my grandmum back in Utah.

I grimaced. This was low, below the belt low. I vowed not to fall for it as I bit into the pie. It was delicious. All it needed was a dollop of ice cream.

But there was no ice cream, and I knew she'd meant it that way,

*knowing I'd want more. I swore I wouldn't let her manipulate me, but I
now knew I had to find this Rosie, whoever she was.*

*I watched as the Widow Wilma Jean got into her stretch Masarati, and
I could see she had dogs. Dogs that were barking. The pink machine drove
off into the black night, the barking fading into the fog.*

———

I t was dawn, and the dogs woke Bud, barking their heads off as
they watched a rabbit in the yard through the patio door.

He was disoriented for a moment, then sighed and went
into the kitchen and made himself a cup of coffee. He put a dollop of
ice cream in the cup, happy it had been just a dream, vowing to quit
reading the book.

After making sure the rabbit was gone, he let the dogs out into the
back yard, taking his coffee out onto the patio.

The dream had been somewhat disturbing, making him wonder
if he really was that easy to manipulate through his stomach. But
after thinking about it for awhile, he decided it didn't really matter
whether he was or not, because the only one who had that kind of
power over him was his wife, and unlike the *Widow* Wilma Jean, the
*real* Wilma Jean had no ulterior motives—at least not that he knew of.

He grinned as he took out his phone. He'd dial the cafe and see if
she could bring him a piece of apple pie when she came home. He
then remembered she was in Radium and the cafe was closed.

He put his phone away and slowly leaned back in the patio chair.
It was then that he realized the dream held a clue—and even though
he wasn't sure if he really understood what it was, it suddenly felt as
if something was shifting, and shifting in a big way.

## 26

Bud sat in his office, fiddling with the little bird point, having taken care of Howie's cats and letting Little Bun out into the yard for the day. He'd taken the dogs for a walk on the farm, then left them in the back yard at the bungalow after having a bowl of cold cereal for breakfast.

Unable to get ahold of either Howie or Wilma Jean, he'd actually called the hospital in Radium, only to be informed that since he wasn't next of kin, they couldn't tell him anything.

He'd finally got ahold of Doc Williams, who'd told him little Malcolm had been born around four that morning and everyone was doing OK. Bud was happy to hear this, knowing they were probably all sleeping and would call him later.

Bud's thoughts now turned to the dream. It had taken some time for him to get rid of the strange feeling it had left behind, one of a teeming city with darkness and mayhem all around. He again thought of Marie—had she been murdered? And why had he felt so strongly upon awakening that the dream held such an obvious clue?

He knew he had a habit of having strange dreams when he was working on a case, dreams that more often than not helped him solve things. He figured it was his subconscious revealing its findings in a dream. He sometimes felt like it was a thing that had its own mind, though he was always happy for the help.

But why a snake? He knew that Wilma Jean and Goldie were maybe symbolic, or could even just be familiar characters who didn't have any meaning in themselves, but the Widow Wilma Jean had said that someone had stolen Rosie's snake, as well as her diary, filling it with locoweed recipes. What in hellsbells would a snake have to do with anything? And why locoweed recipes? Was Rosie short for Rosalind?

And the dream had mentioned the punishment fitting the crime. Did it all have something to do with the sheet music he'd found in the fire ring?

The Widow Wilma Jean did remind him a little of the scene in the book where the private eye was at a fancy restaurant with Jill Thaddeus, but why would that be of any importance? And Pawnshop Goldie had to be Junkyard Goldie—he was from New York, but he'd moved to Green River years ago. He ran a junkyard, not a pawn shop. It didn't make any sense. Bud began wondering if his subconscious had somehow been eating locoweed.

Now Bud's phone was ringing, and he could see it was the Radium County Sheriff's Office.

"Yell-ow"

"Bud, Cal here. How's everything going?"

"Oh, fine. Hows about you?"

"Not so good. We're stuck here in Radium and we need your help."

"What can I do, Cal?"

"Well, we have a report of a couple of Japanese tourists lost out in Yellow Cat Flats, and it seems one of them is diabetic and doesn't have his insulin. Their daughter called us. They were supposed to be back to Radium last night. She's worried and wants us to go find them."

"All night in the Yellow Cat?" Bud asked. "How does she know that's where they went?"

"We called the phone company and their last cell phone call

pinged off the tower up by Cisco. We think they went out the north entrance of the park and got turned around on the Yellow Cat road. They actually called her and said something about an old mine before the signal dropped."

"What are they driving?"

"Some kind of Honda. Dark gray with California plates. Can you get out there?"

"I can, Cal, but I think maybe I should go by the medical clinic here first and get some insulin. Any idea what the guy would need?"

"No idea, but maybe also take something with sugar in case he's going hypoglycemic. They're probably pretty hungry by now, too."

"Yellow Cat's a big place," Bud replied. "But driving a Honda's going to limit where they can go. Are you sure they didn't just go out the north entrance and turn south on the Thompson cutoff? They would've met the highway."

"Well, I guess it's possible, but the highway's closed, so they'd have to go north and would be in Green River by now. Maybe they got a room there, but the daughter said it was totally unlike them to not call. If they were up your way, she thinks they would've called and let her know. Besides, there's no mine out that way."

"Makes sense," Bud said. "I'll run by the clinic and head out right away. I'll call you when I get back."

"Roger and over," Cal said, hanging up.

Bud was soon at the clinic, where he got a vial of insulin and some needles from Dr. Rocky, then he ran by the Melon Harvest and bought some sandwiches, a six-pack of Old Man Green's watermelon spritzer, some apples, and thinking of Jay, a package of red licorice.

He then went to the bungalow and gave Hoppie and Pierre some treats as he slipped Lindie out the door, hoping they wouldn't notice. He was still feeling guilty for not taking them out more, but he wanted to get Lindie used to running around with him. At the last minute, he remembered his harmonica, then his Ruger and holster.

Now in the Land Cruiser, he dialed Shorty's number.

"Shorty, want to go spend some time in the Yellow Cat? I'm going out to look for a couple of lost tourists."

Shorty met Bud at his office, and they were soon in the Land Cruiser, on their way. But instead of going on out to the Yellow Cat exit, Bud decided to turn south at Crescent Junction, then double back on the Thompson cutoff to see if he could find any sign of the lost tourists.

"You happen to check the weather forecast lately?" he asked Shorty.

"No, but it looks pretty good to me," Shorty replied, nodding toward the blue sky overhead.

Bud now asked, "Shorty, do you know anything about opera?"

"Not that I want to remember," Shorty said.

"Does that mean you once did?" Bud persisted.

"My mom listened to it some when I was a kid. I think she was trying to get the family to appreciate classical music."

"Is opera classified as classical?"

"I don't know, but she liked classical, and whenever she'd play opera, my dad, who normally didn't care at all for classical, would tell her to put on some Bach or something. I remember him saying once that opera was a way to slow down time."

"Slow down time?"

"Yeah, he'd say that you could start listening to an opera, say something like La Traviata, and maybe it would start at say, two o'clock. After it had been going about three hours you'd look at your watch and it would say 2:20."

Bud laughed. "You grew up a lot more educated musically than I did. About the only music we had was the local radio station and when my dad tried to play old cowboy songs on his guitar."

"Tried?"

"He had a few songs down pretty good, and he just played them over and over. That's part of why he had them down, he never tried anything new. But have you ever heard any opera lyrics that have something to do with making the punishment fit the crime?"

"That's from Gilbert and Sullivan," Shorty replied. "My mom loved them. I think she knew all the lyrics to everything they wrote. I'm not sure their stuff would be classified as opera, but maybe more as operetta. They were Brits, back in the 1800s, and that's from the Mikado. I can't recall the plot, but the lyrics go something like, *My object all sublime, I shall achieve in time, To let the punishment fit the crime.* It's actually a pretty famous line. They're considered the fathers of the musical."

"Do you have any idea why someone would burn the sheet music in a campfire?" Bud asked.

"Maybe they hated Gilbert and Sullivan—or maybe they just needed some kindle," Shorty replied. "But it's probably not real common to carry around the sheet music to the Mikado."

They were now on the back road into the Yellow Cat, the same one that met with the back entrance to the national park. Bud could now see a vehicle coming toward them, and he slowed.

He could soon make out an old army ambulance, and he knew it had to be Jasper and Leon, probably on their way to gathering material for another "espeedode" of the K-RAT Show, helping themselves to tourist goodies.

He pulled over and waited, hoping they would stop, and as they got closer, he thought he could see a couple of heads through a window in the back. He wondered if they'd somehow recruited accomplices.

He thought about turning on his flashing lights, but he figured that would just make them go faster or maybe turn around and go the opposite direction, so he just waited.

They soon arrived, bringing a cloud of swirling dust with them.

## 27

---

"Howdy, Sheriff," Leon said, half-hanging out the ambulance window. "Lookin' for somebody?"

"Morning," Bud replied. "Actually, I am."

"Would it happen to be a couple of tourists?" Leon asked. "I have a nice pair here you can have. They need some chow and medical attention, so we were going to take them down to Radium, but we're a little low on gas."

"The highway's closed down there," Bud replied. "The bridge is about to go out. The sheriff's office called and asked us to come out and find them. If they're the same couple, the fellow needs some insulin."

Bud and Shorty got out as Leon opened the back door to the ambulance, helping the couple out. The man looked pale and weak. Bud handed the insulin and needles to the man's wife, as well as the sandwiches and drinks.

Now Shorty asked Jasper, "You know any Japanese?"

Jasper, looking surprised, asked, "Why in hellsbells would I know any Japanese?"

Shorty grinned. "I thought maybe you learned some when you

were in the 10th Mountain Division. You know, maybe when you were down in the South Pacific Theater in World War II?"

Jasper shook his head in irritation. "Whattya think the *mountain* in 10th Mountain Division means? Mountains, my friend, not islands."

Shorty replied, "There's some pretty good mountains on some of those islands." He continued to grin as he helped Bud get the pair into the Land Cruiser, Lindie jumping into the front.

Now Bud, noting how Jasper and Leon had eyed the sandwiches, took out the ones he'd bought for him and Shorty and handed them to Leon.

"We're not going to need these, since we're heading right back to Green River. Maybe you can serve them up to yourselves out at the Yellow Cat Cafe." He then took out the red licorice. "And if you see Jay, give this red licorice to him."

Leon, looking suspicious, said, "How'd you know he's with us?"

Bud was surprised. "With you? Where?"

Jay now came out of the back of the ambulance, saying, "Did I hear my name and red licorice in the same sentence? Can I get a ride with you guys to Green River?"

"Where's your Jeep?" Bud asked.

Acting as if he didn't want to talk about it, Jay finally said, "It appears to have been stolen."

Leon now whispered confidentially, "Aliens, like I told you. Jasper thinks I'm nuts, but who else could pull off something like that, stealing vehicles out in the middle of nowhere without being seen?"

Jasper, who had obviously heard him, said, "It's easy to not be seen when there's nobody around, Leon. Aliens is the stupidest idea I've ever heard. But whoever took Jay's Jeep also took this couple's car." He turned to Bud and said, "We found them walking down the road late last night."

"How do you know their car was stolen if you can't speak Japanese?" Shorty asked.

"Why else would they be walking down the road?" Jasper replied with frustration. "Some things are just obvious. And why would I need to know Japanese?"

"It's aliens," Leon added. "Their car's probably way up high on some cliff in the Books. We took them back to the cafe and fed them some Dinty Moore canned stew, then we gave them our cots and slept out in the ambulance. They seem like nice people, but we could tell the fellow wasn't feeling too good. We fed him some canned peaches and that seemed to help."

"Well, that was really nice of you," Bud replied. "But we need to get him up to the clinic and make sure he's OK. Jay, you mind riding way in the back with Lindie?"

"You have anything else we can serve at the cafe?" Leon asked hopefully.

Bud handed Leon the bag of apples he'd bought, then said, "If you fellows are short of gas, you might want to skip the national park. I have a feeling it's gonna be slim pickings with the road to Radium closed. Won't be anyone out there."

Leon smiled. "Sure is nice of the sheriff to give us an update on the state of tourist accessibles at the national park."

Bud shook his head as everyone loaded up, and they were soon on their way to Green River, Jasper and Leon continuing on toward the park. Bud could see the Japanese fellow in his rear-view mirror, and it appeared that he was doing better, acting a little perkier.

Bud now thought of Howie and Maureen and the baby, wondering when Wilma Jean would call him. Surely they were up and about by now.

Back in town, Bud dropped the couple off at the clinic, explaining the situation to the nurse. He then called Molly at the Melon View B&B to get them a room there. He'd have Hum call their daughter.

Now he asked Jay, "Where are we taking you?"

Jay replied, "I don't know. I need to call the rental company and tell them their Jeep's been stolen, then somehow get down there and get my car, which is in their parking lot. But since the road's closed, I guess I need a motel room, but when I was here last, there wasn't a room to be found anywhere because of the rock show."

"Let me call and see if there's room at my wife's B&B," Bud said.

He talked a few minutes to Molly, then said, "She's all booked up. But you could come stay in our Airstream."

Now Shorty said, "Bud, he can stay at my farm. The house is just sitting there empty. It's a little roomier than your trailer."

"I really don't want to put anyone out," Jay said thoughtfully. "But I kind of need to reconnoiter and figure out where to go from here. All my clothes and everything were in that Jeep. I'll need a ride to Radium to get my car at some point."

It now occurred to Bud that Jay probably still didn't know that his ex-wife, Marie, was dead, but he knew this wasn't the best time to tell him.

Bud said, "After I get this couple settled in, we can go on out to Shorty's. You'll need to get some groceries first. If you want, we can stop by the thrift store for some clothes. We'll work on getting you to Radium when the road opens back up."

Now Shorty said, "Bud, drop us off at my truck and I'll take him out there. You have your hands full. You can come out later."

"Sounds like a plan," Bud replied, soon dropping them off at his office, where Shorty had parked his truck.

Just then, Wilma Jean called, and he got the complete rundown on everything, including how Howie had rocked little Malcolm for hours while Maureen slept, singing him tunes from their band, Howie and the Road Rangers. All the nurses and doctors had come by to listen at one time or another.

Bud laughed, relieved. He'd go pick up the Japanese couple, take them to the B&B, then go check on the dogs at the bungalow and have some lunch.

As he drove back to the clinic, he could picture Howie rocking tiny little Malcolm, singing:

> I'm down to my last wad of chew.
> And honey, you know I'm sure blue.
> You walked out on me,

And you took my car key,
And I'm down to my last wad of chew.

## 28

Bud had just taken the dogs for a nice walk around one of the big melon fields, and he could see his farm manager, Kale, off in the distance plowing, raising dust that looked like it was headed for Shorty's place.

It was one of the main problems with having a B&B on a farm, Bud mused, for he'd heard both Wilma Jean and Molly complain about having to endlessly dust to keep things nice for the guests. He figured it was a good thing he wasn't running the lodging part of things, as he considered dust as just part of the farm-stay experience.

He could see across the fields to where Shorty's pickup sat in front of his house, and Bud knew he was still there with Jay. Maybe they were talking opera, Bud grinned, or worse, singing it.

Throwing a stick for the dogs, Bud now thought back on his dream, again wondering why he'd thought it had held an important clue. He'd decided that the reason Wilma Jean was in the dream was from reading about Jill Thaddeus in the book, all elegant and well-dressed and such, and his subconscious had handily substituted his wife, who did have a touch of panache, though she seemed much more trustworthy than Jill. But why Junkyard Goldie, who'd been called Pawnshop Goldie?

He knew Goldie had nothing to do with Marie's death—had he been in the dream simply because he was from New York and had a beard like Jay? Bud suspected this was the case, but he now felt he needed to go talk to him to help adjust things back to reality. There was no way Goldie would get involved in anything like Marie's death, and Bud was sure Goldie had never even met her. But Goldie was kind of a big guy, just like Jay, so maybe there was some substitution going on there.

He loaded the dogs into the FJ, dropped Hoppie and Pierre off at the bungalow, then headed for Goldie's junkyard, which was on the other side of the river in the part of town once known as Elgin.

Once there, he saw a closed sign, the big metal gate around the compound locked shut. He knew Goldie spent a lot of time at Old Man Green's nearby farm, so Bud headed over there.

Bud was surprised to see not just Goldie's car, but also Eldon and Frosty's old Jeeps parked in front of Old Man Green's big farmhouse. As he got closer, he could see a number of people sitting in chairs on the big grassy lawn under the giant elms, which were just starting to green up.

As he got out, Goldie yelled, "Hey Sheriff, come on over and have some watermelon spritzer! We need another opinion!"

Bud grinned as he noted Mrs. Jensen was also there, sitting next to Frosty, her hand on his, Frosty looking embarrassed and Eldon sitting nearby, as if keeping an eye on the pair.

Goldie added, "We're having a business meeting and maybe you can give us some ideas, seeing how you and your wife are business types."

Bud replied, "Goldie, Wilma Jean's the one you want to talk to, not me. I pretty much just go along for the ride."

He nodded at Mrs. Jensen as Old Man Green said, "It's more like a 'Goldie wants to have a business' meeting, not me. He's already got a business, his old junkyard. And we ain't going nowhere without an angel."

"What in hellsbells does an angel have to do with anything?"

Eldon asked testily. "You think some angel's gonna drop a gazillion dollars on your head out of the blue?"

Now Frosty patiently replied, "Eldon, you sure don't know anything about business. An angel is what they call an investor. It's not a religious thing."

"Seems like we need to get a bit more religious if we want to see this thing off the ground," Eldon replied. "Do some hard-core prayin', though drinkin' that dang hard watermelon spritzer's a religious experience, for sure." He glanced at Bud, adding, "Not that we have any of that evil stuff around."

Bud laughed. "You know it's OK to make it, just not to sell it. You can sit here and drink it all day if you want, just don't go driving anywhere. But if you don't mind me asking, why do you need an investor?"

Now Old Man Green spoke up. "We don't. It's all Goldie's idea. I'm happy just selling the non-alcoholic stuff. Me and Goldie bottle up a few dozen bottles for sale every week then sell it over at the Melon Harvest and make enough to cover our gambling debts, and that's good enough for me. No need to get greedy and wanna be a big tycoon. Besides, we're going to get shut down if the Board of Health ever asks to see our facility."

"Nothing wrong with that barn," Goldie said, annoyed. "But you sure don't look to the future, do you?"

"That's 'cause I'm not sure I have one," Old Man Green replied. "You, neither, Goldie. We ain't spring chickens anymore, you know."

"Gambling debts?" Bud grinned. "You boys aren't playing poker over here when I'm not looking, are you?"

"Bingo," Goldie replied. "We go over to the church on Fridays and play bingo."

Old Man Green snorted, but didn't say anything.

Finally, Frosty said, "Eileen here has something she wants to say, if the chair will just recognize her."

Goldie said, "The chair recognizes Mrs. Jensen. Go ahead, Eileen, speak your mind. We won't interrupt."

Now Mrs. Jensen said, "I'll be your angel. I'd be willing to invest to help you get going, as long as you sign a legal contract so I know I'll get it back."

Now everyone was silent. Finally, Goldie asked, "Just how much would you be willing to invest?"

"Well," she replied. "It's not much, but I have a little from my husband's life insurance. I'd be willing to put in say, maybe around a thousand dollars."

"A thousand dollars?" Goldie asked. "That's a fortune! We could set up a whole bottling enterprise with that, right, Green?"

But Old Man Green wasn't listening, for he'd suddenly abandoned his lawn chair and was headed into the house.

"I guess he's not interested," Frosty said, looking at Mrs. Jensen with new eyes. "That was really nice of you, Eileen, but I don't think he's ready."

"Give him some time," Goldie said. "Meeting adjourned."

"He's gonna need lots of time," Eldon added, scowling. "You guys need to forget this business stuff. Come on out with the BOB-Os and have some fun. We're setting up a trip out to Hastings Canyon to look at petroglyphs. Mrs. Jensen's coming along, aren't you, dear?"

Frosty now had a hunted look as she replied, "I wouldn't miss it for anything."

"This really entertains you, doesn't it, Eldon?" Frosty whispered under his breath.

"You have no idea," Eldon replied, laughing.

"What entertains him?" Mrs. Jensen asked.

"Oh, just life in general," Eldon replied, standing. "Looks like the meeting's over, so we might as well go get some lunch. You have any more of those delicious chicken-salad sandwiches over at your place, Eileen?"

As they left, Bud took Goldie aside and asked, "Goldie, you have a minute? I need to ask you a couple of questions."

"We're not playing poker, Bud, in spite of what you might think."

Bud laughed. "Goldie, you know I don't care what you guys do in the privacy of your home."

"We play in Green's barn, not his home," Goldie replied. "Right after Sherwyn down at the Melon Harvest pays us for the spritzer. We split the money, then play poker. I usually win. Makes Green mad as a hornet."

"Goldie, I need to ask you if you've ever met a gal from New York. She was driving a little red sportster. Did she ever come by your junk-yard or anything?"

"Yes, I remember her," Goldie replied. "Is she in some kind of trouble? She was kind of hard to forget, wanting to see if I had some kind of jack that would work for her car. She's the kind of person we need as an investor, Bud. Anyone driving a Shelby Cobra has some hard, cold cash—assuming they didn't spend it all on the car."

Bud nodded his head, trying to take in what Goldie had just told him, but having a hard time getting it to register. The little red sport-ster was a Shelby Cobra? He thought of the snake in his dream.

After recovering his equilibrium and thanking Goldie, Bud decided he needed to go talk to Shorty.

## 29

Bud headed to Shorty's farm, wondering how he'd missed the fact that the two roadsters he'd seen were expensive and rare Cobras.

Maybe it was because they were expensive and rare, he mused, knowing that either of those two criteria would exclude him, yet alone both together. He was happy with his FJ, for it would take him wherever he wanted to go, and he didn't need a special jack for it, either. He just didn't pay that much attention to vehicles he never saw.

He now thought back to the passage in Marie's book where Nails the biker was loading a Shelby Cobra into a truck, one he'd stolen and had presumably just painted. Had Marie intended for it to be some kind of clue, or had she written about it only because she had one and it was something she was familiar with? And hadn't the character Jill said Nails was her ex-husband? Was Nails supposed to be Jay?

Now Bud turned into Shorty's drive, letting Lindie out, who went straight to the front door. Shorty had seen them coming, for he opened the door, and Lindie went inside.

As Bud came to the door, Shorty said quietly, "By the way, Bud, are you aware that Jay was just named Opera Singer of the Year by *Time Magazine*?"

"No, I didn't know that," Bud replied. "You get *Time*?"

"No, I read it down at the stand in the grocery store when we got groceries. I'm not even sure Jay noticed. I bought a copy, but I haven't shown it to him yet."

Bud said, "Maybe he doesn't know about it. It sounds pretty prestigious. I still wish I knew what the heck he's doing out here."

"Come on in. You might as well stay for lunch. Jay's going to make a big batch of lasagna—he says he likes to cook."

Bud replied, "It sounds really good, but I need to get some things done."

"It's OK," Shorty said. "We'll save you some. I've been showing Jay the house. He seems really impressed, much more so than I would expect someone from New York City to be. You know, there's some pretty ritzy stuff back there."

Bud knew that Shorty was just like him, impressed more by the works of nature than by the works of man.

"I would assume there's for sure some nice stuff out there," Bud replied. "Given they say it's the center of their financial world."

"But not of *our* financial world, eh?" Shorty laughed.

"Nah, mine's more like Wilma Jean's purse," Bud grinned. "Especially since I give her my paycheck every month. But Shorty, I need to tell Jay that his ex-wife's dead."

"Not going to be much fun," Shorty replied. "Come on in."

They were soon out in Shorty's back yard, Lindie trying to get Bud to play with an old ball she'd found. Bud ignored her, as it was matted with dead grass and dirt, so she finally went to Shorty, who kicked it to Jay, who then kicked it into the corner of the yard.

"I love this place," Jay said, sipping a cup of tea. "I could live here."

"Nah, you'd go nuts out here, being from New York and all," Shorty replied. "The peace and quiet would drive you crazy."

Jay looked hurt for a moment, then said, "Not true, but I wouldn't know how I'd make a living here, anyway. But I would love to live here."

"Not much of a demand for opera out here," Bud replied. "Though we did have a Shakespearean troop come through once."

"What's Shakespeare got to do with opera?" Shorty asked.

"He probably associates it all with high-brow stuff," Jay said, again kicking the ball Lindie had dropped at his feet. "And it kind of is, to be honest."

"Nonsense," Shorty replied. "I hum the Barber of Seville all the time. Gilbert and Sullivan, too. They're an integral part of my ability to cope with life."

He started singing:

> My object all sublime,
> I shall achieve in time,
> To let the punishment fit the crime,
> The punishment fit the crime.
> And make each prisoner pent,
> Unwillingly represent,
> A source of innocent merriment!
> Of innocent merriment!

Bud watched Jay's reaction—had he been the one who'd burned the sheet music?

"It's rare to meet someone who knows the lyrics to the Mikado," Jay said. "I was really getting into Gilbert and Sullivan, but my ex-wife hated them, so I dropped it. But they were a lot of fun, especially when coming off things like Wagner's *Das Rheingold*."

Shorty said, "You know, Mark Twain once said that there isn't anything in Wagner opera that one would call by such a violent name as acting. I kind of agree."

"So you're saying opera requires acting?" Bud asked.

"Well," Jay replied. "Some say opera is acting through singing. After all, you do have a plot and all that, like any kind of story."

"And there's plenty of drama," Shorty mused. "But I've always admired how opera singers can sing in so many foreign languages, how they can translate *la-la-la-la* into German or Italian or whatever and it's still perfectly understandable."

Jay laughed, kicking the ball again.

Now Shorty said, "Jay, are you aware that you were just named Opera Singer of the Year by *Time Magazine*?"

Jay looked startled. "You're kidding, right?"

Shorty took the magazine from the counter and handed it to Jay, who was speechless. He finally said, "This isn't one of those things you can have made up as a gag, is it?"

"Nope, it's the real deal," Shorty said. "Congrats."

Bud added, "Yes, congratulations. I never thought I'd meet Time's Opera Singer of the Year." The reality was, Bud thought, before Jay, he'd never thought he'd ever meet an opera singer of any kind.

Jay sat in silence, then said, "This will be a big boost to my career, though I'm not sure I want a boost. I've been thinking of changing professions."

Bud said, "Maybe you should go into regular singing. I heard you did a really good Willy Nelson concert on the K-RAT Show, though I wasn't lucky enough to hear it in person."

Jay replied, "That was a lot of fun. Those guys are a couple of characters, but they ate all my red licorice—and the fudge I bought in that tourist shop—and my road cookies."

Now Shorty asked, "Who do you think stole your Jeep?"

Jay looked thoughtful, then said, "Leon told me there's been a rash of stolen vehicles out there."

"Do you know someone driving a Shelby Cobra?" Bud now asked. "Did it also get stolen?"

Now Jay looked flummoxed. "I don't think it was stolen, was it? I actually don't know."

Bud said quietly, "Jay, I hate to bring you bad news, especially on the heels of such an achievement, but the Radium County Sheriff's Office found Marie Lee's body out in the Yellow Cat a couple of days ago. I'm really sorry."

Jay involuntarily touched his neck, and Bud noticed that his shirt collar was turned up as if trying to hide what looked like some kind of rash or bruise. Jay said nothing, Lindie waiting for him to again kick the ball. When he finally spoke, Bud was surprised at his answer.

"Sheriff Shumway, do you have an autopsy report to prove that?"

Jay now kicked the ball for Lindie, and as it again went into the far corner of Shorty's yard, Bud could see Kale in the distance, still plowing.

He suddenly wished he was the one on the tractor, far away from anything to do with Jay, Marie Lee, and *The Last Opera Show*, for he was beginning to think he would never be able to figure it all out.

# 30

---

Bud was confused. Jay hadn't reacted to the news that Marie was dead at all like he'd expected, and he was now engrossed in the article in *Time*. Bud wanted to ask him more questions, but didn't want to spoil his moment of fame and happiness, though Jay didn't look very happy.

Bud was suddenly tired. He needed to call Hum down in Radium and check on things back at the office. He also wanted to see if he could get ahold of Wilma Jean or Howie. He knew that, unless Jay was suddenly more forthcoming than he'd been before, he wouldn't answer his questions anyway.

Bud said goodbye to Shorty and Jay, then headed for the bungalow, again feeling guilty for leaving the boys so much. They were happy to see him, and he played stick with them for awhile, then loaded everyone up and went to the office.

He hadn't been there more than 10 minutes when a small blonde man came to the door. He was scruffy looking, and Bud figured he was a rockhound, especially since he was carrying a beat-up daypack that looked as if it held something heavy.

"Excuse me," the man said, sticking his head in the door. "It says *Sheriff's Office*, but this looks like the dog pound. Can you point me in the right direction?"

Bud laughed. "This is the sheriff's office. Don't mind the dogs, they're just in temporary detainment for chasing bunnies. I'll let them go as soon as I can write them all tickets. Come on in."

The man came in, petting Lindie, who had gone to greet him. Pierre and Hoppie were busy chewing on rawhide sticks Bud had given them, but Lindie had already wolfed hers down.

"What can I do for you?" Bud asked, motioning for the man to have a seat.

The man sat down, then said, "My name is Paul Devlin. I'm with the Dirty Dogs Rockhound Club. We're here for the rock show. I just wanted to let someone know what we found."

Bud said, "Go ahead, Mr. Devlin. I'm listening."

"Call me Paul. Well, we were out in Yellow Cat Flats, looking for petrified redwood. It's legal to hunt it, you know."

"I know, I have a few pieces myself," Bud replied, trying to reassure the guy. He was getting kind of tired of everyone always assuming he was going to try to arrest them for something or other, as if he didn't have anything better to do.

Paul, now seeming to relax, began waxing eloquent about the beauties of petrified redwood and how nice the cabs were once it was all polished up. He then started praising the agates out there, and told Bud how he'd even found some dinosaur coprolites.

Bud leaned back, half-listening, thinking that maybe he should start a ride-along program to give people a feel for what he actually did each day so they wouldn't think all he did was arrest people. After all, there was the cattle in the road kind of thing and all the calls wanting him to do something about the potholes in town, as well as Mrs. Jensen calling about kids trespassing on her lawn. Now thinking about it, he decided he owed Frosty Merriott a big thank you for distracting her, as they hadn't had a call from her for some time.

Now Paul was talking about the roads in the Yellow Cat and how they often led to nowhere, but how that was perfect for rock-hounding, and how they'd found this place where crystal-filled logs stuck out of a big cliff and it was called the Parade of Logs and how they'd almost got stuck there.

Bud was now beginning to think Paul might be related to Howie, having the same propensity for taking his time getting to the subject at hand.

As Paul continued, even taking some agate from his pack and showing him, Bud thought again about the ride-along. Maybe it wasn't such a good idea, for nothing ever happened in Green River, and if people hung out with him all day, they might just decide a full-time sheriff wasn't really necessary, especially since he was actually now covering cases not even in his county.

Finally, in an attempt to get Paul back on track, Bud interrupted, saying, "You do know the Yellow Cat District isn't part of my jurisdiction, don't you? It's in Radium County."

"I know that, Sheriff, but we can't get to Radium, as there's a big 'road closed' sign off the freeway."

"What exactly did you want to report?" Bud asked.

"Before I forget, is there a rock shop here?" Paul asked.

"No, the nearest one is Ernie Shirley's place down in Hanksville."

"Well, let me show you something, Sheriff." Paul now pulled something from his pocket and handed it to Bud, who whistled. It was a petrified red pinecone, maybe all of an inch long and with perfect detail.

"This is a first for me," Bud replied, holding it up and examining it. "You think it's from a redwood tree?"

"It very well could be," Paul replied, beaming. "I'm going to donate it to the museum over in Grand Junction."

"Well, it's a beauty," Bud said, wondering if this is what the guy had wanted to tell him about. It was a nice find, very rare, but not something most people would consider taking to show the local sheriff.

"You know, I'm going to quit my job and come over here and stake a claim on this stuff," Paul informed Bud. "I found what looks to be a very productive redwood location."

"How can you stake a claim on petrified wood when it's illegal to take over 25 pounds?" Bud asked, thinking of Jasper and Leon's meteorite claim. "Is it on state lands?"

"No, it's BLM, and no, you can't stake a claim on petrified wood. But I called them, and they told me that redwood limb casts are not considered petrified wood because there's no visible grain structure. It's considered agate. So I'm going to stake a claim on 'Rare and Unusual Agate,' which is perfectly legal."

"Well, Paul, that's all well and good, and since you're not in my jurisdiction anyway, you know I wouldn't bother you. Besides, I don't work for the BLM. Maybe once the road opens you should call the Radium sheriff and tell them, though they wouldn't bother you, either."

"Oh, I'm not worried about that, Sheriff," Paul replied. "And I'm sorry I got so excited about all this. I didn't mean to. But I just can't wait to get back and stake my claim. I'm a bit excited."

"I think that's great," Bud said, now feeling a little restless, wanting to get on the phone and call Hum. He was wondering if they'd got the coroner's report back, plus he wanted to know what Hum would suggest about recovering the Japanese couple's car, if they could find it.

"Oh, and I almost forgot," Paul added. "I need to tell you that someone stole a bunch of our camping equipment."

"Out in the Yellow Cat?"

"Yeah, we were camped over by the Ringtail Mine. They came into our camp while we were out rockhounding and took most of our food and water. They left a day's worth, so that was considerate of them, at least."

Bud groaned. He'd been avoiding it, but he knew someone was going to have to talk to Jasper and Leon. The pair had told him that stealing cars was going to lead to someone dying, but so was stealing people's food and water.

"OK, let's do a formal report, then I can fax it to the Radium Sheriff, since you can't get down there."

"It's OK," Paul said. "We figure if someone's going to steal stuff like that, they must need it more than we do. At least they didn't take our nice camp chairs and tents. We'll just be more careful next time."

Bud now wondered why Paul had come in, if not to make a report.

Paul said, "That's not why I came in here, though it would be nice if something could be done about that. But, Sheriff, I found this out by the Ringtail Mine. It was hanging on a bush right by the road."

He then pulled an elegant red silk jacket from his pack and handed it to Bud, saying, "It was hung on a rabbitbrush. It doesn't look to me like anything anyone I know would wear, especially since it's a woman's. I went through the pockets, trying to find out if there was an ID or something, and I found this, which is why I came in here. Sheriff, it's kind of disturbing. I hope I didn't mess up any fingerprints or anything by opening it up."

Paul handed Bud a small envelope made from what looked to be expensive linen stationary, with the letters "R.L." embossed in red on the back.

Bud carefully opened it, and inside was a note, also on an expensive-looking linen paper. It had the same handwriting as the notebook he'd found with "Rosalind Lee" written over and over in it.

Bud read:

Marie, I hate to tell you this, but I have concrete evidence that Jay is out to kill you. He's going to get you out in the Utah desert under the pretense of some kind of new pigment for your art, then murder you there and steal your Cobra. Please, please don't go. Love, Rosie.

"Maybe it's some kind of joke, Sheriff," Paul said, looking grim.

"I wish it were, Paul, but I think it's for real," Bud replied. "Thanks for taking the time to bring this in. What you just gave me could very well help me figure out something that's been keeping me up at night."

With that, they both stood, shook hands, and Paul went out the door, Bud thinking of how the Widow Wilma Jean in his dream had mentioned Rosie and how Rosie had to be Rosalind, Marie's sister.

# 31

Bud now pushed his chair back, thinking. Did the jacket belong to Rosalind? The initials on the stationary indicated that was a good possibility, and the note was signed from her, but hadn't Rosalind been dressed in black when she'd come into the cafe?

Maybe she'd put the jacket on later, which Bud knew wouldn't be at all unusual. But if it was her jacket, it would put her in the same area as Marie. Did she have something to do with Marie's death?

Bud was beginning to feel confused, and now Jay Landowska had added to the confusion by acting like he wasn't very concerned about Marie being dead and out in the Yellow Cat. Maybe he was glad to see her gone, Bud mused.

Bud was tired. It had been a long day, and he wanted nothing more than to just go home and relax. He loaded the dogs up and headed for the bungalow, stopping on the way at the Melon Harvest Grocery to get a TV dinner.

Back home, he fed the dogs and then heated up the dinner, eating it on the back patio. While browsing through one of Wilma Jean's aviation magazines, he tried to call her, but he got no answer. He knew he should just go to bed and get some rest, but he felt uneasy.

Finally, after pacing around for awhile, Bud turned on his

computer. He felt like he'd been lax in his research, and he needed to find out more about Marie Lee. The calls he'd intended to make would wait.

He'd keyed in *Marie Lee author* on his earlier search, but this time he instead keyed in *Marie Lee painter*. He was surprised when he got several pages of hits, all from what looked to be fairly reputable sources. He clicked on the first, which was an article in *Metropolitan Art*, and read:

> *New York Artist Creates Sustainable Art*
>
> When well-known artist Marie Lee sets about to begin a new project, she doesn't start by gathering the conventional tools most artists use, such as canvas and oils, but instead goes for a walk in Central Park. It's there she finds her inspiration in the trees and flowers, especially those with unusual shades.
>
> Lee's work is highly valued by collectors for its unique colors, using hues rarely seen together in more traditional art, for Lee seems to completely disregard all theories about the color wheel and complimentary colors. Yet it all comes together in stunning pieces that are pleasing to the eye, and her impressionistic style is one of a kind.
>
> "I used to work with traditional oils," Lee says, "Until I realized how harmful they were to the environment. I've always tried to portray what I believe, and for me, using natural pigments is very important. I get all my tints from nature and avoid toxic ingredients. I mix my own own paints using a special biodegradable blend of egg yolk, water, and pigments I personally collect from natural settings. I'll travel any distance to obtain a color I want to incorporate into my work. All natural ingredients are especially important to me since I have a rare hereditary disease that makes me very sensitive to any kind of chemicals."
>
> Lee's latest piece is called "To Preserve and Protect" and features a line of purple and orange German Shepherd police dogs standing obediently at alert as a green cat crosses in front of them. The painting was purchased by the Blue Line, a consortium of law-enforcement officers in the Bronx, and will hang in their headquarters. Lee preferred not to disclose the price,

*but says she'll be sponsoring their float in this year's St. Patrick's Day parade.*

Bud thought he'd maybe seen that painting somewhere, or was it a photo?

After reading several other articles about Marie, all which touted her painting skills, Bud then did a search on *Kelso guide book*.

All he knew about the guy was what Leon had told him when he and Shorty were at the Yellow Cat Cafe, which was that he was a rascal and always got everyone lost, doing all the research for his guide books on Google Earth.

Bud's search brought back a number of links to books, all with titles like *Kelso's Guide to Hiking Utah's Fabulous Canyons* or *Kelso's Guide to Hiking Utah's Fabulous National Parks*. He finally saw one called *Kelso's Guide to Rockhounding the Fabulous Yellow Cat District*.

The link took him to a webpage for the book with a preview:

*With names like the Parade of Logs, Coprolite Ridge, Valley of the Giant Crayons, and the Big Old Carnotite Log, it's hard to go wrong out in Utah's Yellow Cat District, a rockhounder's paradise (and bring your pebble pups).*

*Yellow Cat Flats is a historic uranium-mining district famous for its brilliant agatized redwood limb casts, as well as many other mineral and fossil finds, such as various types of agates, barite pseudomorphs, petrified wood, Sanchez jasper, and pigeon blood agate. Bring a big pack, because you'll need it! Redwood limb casts from the Yellow Cat can sell for thousands of dollars to collectors, so maybe you'll even get rich!*

*The area is extremely desolate, and there's no water (all ground water is contaminated with uranium and arsenic), no food, and sporadic cell phone service (only when you can see the Salt Mountains). Even though you're only 10 to 20 miles from the interstate, you're extremely isolated from the rest of civilization, but the tradeoff is the scenery. With hills and buttes resembling the Painted Desert in Arizona and beautiful views of the nearby national park, you'll be hard pressed to leave.*

*Best of all, the area can easily be accessed with a standard passenger car, and there's no need for a high-clearance vehicle. It's good driving even in rain and snow, and the roads are easy to follow and not get lost.*

*But if you do end up having problems, keep this number handy: Tanner Towing and Off-Road Recovery, 435-259-8825, 24-hour service. And remember, if you don't have cell service, just climb a big hill.*

Bud shook his head, thinking of how prophetic the line *you'll be hard pressed to leave* was—you definitely would, because Tex Tanner would come and tow your car away.

The big question was, did Tanner actually steal the cars for resale or just tow them to his lot and demand ransom before he would release them? And was Kelso in on the game with him or was just innocently giving people the number of a tow service in case they got stuck?

It seemed to Bud that Kelso was setting people up for Tanner's services, for anyone who'd ever been in the Yellow Cat knew you needed high clearance and that the roads were impassible when wet. It was also easy to get lost, for tracks headed off everywhere from the main roads. Of course, if Kelso did all his research on the Internet, maybe he was just winging it and didn't actually know that.

Bud now continued his search, looking at other links, several which linked Kelso's name with search-and-rescue operations. He found a discussion on a climbing forum that was interesting:

*Lost in Utah: I know Mitt Kelso personally, and he says he actually hikes and climbs everything in his books, but I know if anything goes wrong, he refuses to accept blame. But all guidebooks are guides, by definition. You always have to be responsible for yourself.*

*Rockskipper: Tell that to the troop of boy scouts he misled into thinking the Black Box was a Sunday stroll. They had to be rescued from that 600-foot deep section where it's nothing but icy water, and some of them were barely alive. Most of the people I've talked to feel like Kelso isn't just spreading misinformation, but is eventually going to get someone killed.*

*Lost in Utah: Agreed. He can't get a real publisher so publishes the books himself. His elderly mother up in Salt Lake does his shipping while he's out galavanting around, supposedly researching. You can't tell me he's been on top of the Fickle Finger of Fate, yet my SAR group had to rescue two climbers up there who were following his directions. We ended up having to get a chopper to haul them out. And he said it was an easy climb in his book, Kelso's Guide to Climbing Utah's Fabulous Towers. He apparently just made the route up. I'm amazed he hasn't been sued.*

*Rockskipper: He has, but he always gets off because of all the caveats he puts in his books. He somehow keeps getting away with it.*

*Lost in Utah: He won't get away with it when some dead person's spouse or parent comes looking for him with a weapon.*

The discussion continued, but Bud had seen all he needed to know.

It appeared that, when dealing with Kelso, the phrase *you'll be hard pressed to leave* referred not only to losing your car, but maybe also to losing your life.

He thought of the body Hum and Cal had retrieved, and wondered if Kelso had somehow been involved. It was maybe time to call Hum and see if the coroner's report had come back, plus he wanted to get a copy of the 911 call.

Bud was ready to turn off the computer when he noticed he had an email. It was from Jody, the search-and-rescue dog trainer over in Colorado. It was a note telling him a few things about training Lindie, so he printed it out, shutting the computer down. He'd read it in more detail in the morning when he wasn't so tired.

After putting on his Scooby Doo PJs, he decided to take the dogs out in the back yard for a few minutes. After all, he grinned, any reputable dog pound had the responsibility of letting its prisoners out into the exercise yard once in awhile.

While the dogs sniffed around for rabbits, Bud leaned back and looked at the stars glittering through the big globe willow, wondering what was going on out in the Yellow Cat at that very moment—probably not much, except for coyotes howling and yellow cats prowling.

He gathered the dogs and went inside, glad to be home.

# 32

It was morning, and Bud had slept much better than he'd thought he would. He made himself some coffee, then sat down to read Jody's email from the night before.

*Bud, here are the few tips I said I'd send over to help you train Lindie. Training a good SAR dog requires positivity, passion, and tons of patience and will take around 600 hours. You have to socialize them, keep them in good shape with lots of exercise, get them used to loud noises (helicopters, etc.), teach them to follow a scent, and also train yourself (be in shape and be aware they can sense your feelings).*

*The basic commands are: find it (begin the search for a human scent), over (climb over an obstacle), tunnel (crawl through a tunnel), leave it (ignore a distraction), and show me (take the trainer to whatever they found).*

*The first step in training is to figure out a good reward and always immediately reward Lindie when she does the right thing. One way to start is to allow her to smell your clothing and then hide in another room. Have another person say find it, and when she finds you, reward her and play a little.*

*There are other methods, but this will be a start. The main thing is to make it fun for her. Good luck and feel free to call if I can help. Jody*

Bud leaned back, thinking. His attempt at having Lindie find Shorty by showing her his hat had actually been on track, but he'd kind of skipped a few steps, namely, getting her used to the command and knowing what he wanted her to do.

He now thought about what Jody's letter said regarding training oneself and being in shape. He hadn't thought about it, but it made sense, since the trainer had to follow the dog around and give her commands and all.

He now felt a bit disappointed in himself. Wilma Jean had been after him for some time to lose a little weight, but he just couldn't reconcile it with her good cooking. He'd actually lost some while up in the Yukon, but he was gradually putting it back on, and if he was serious about training Lindie to be a SAR dog, he'd have to change his eating habits, which he wasn't so sure he could do. Maybe he could just start exercising more.

He now thought back to his dream and the Widow Wilma Jean bringing him a piece of apple pie. He knew he needed to stop eating stuff like that, and maybe if he started putting a little milk in his coffee instead of dollops of ice cream that would also help, but it would be a hard row to hoe.

He took out his phone and dialed the number for the Radium County Sheriff.

"Sheriff's office, Deputy Cal Murphy speaking."

"Hey Cal, it's Bud. How are things going down your way?"

"Oh, hello there, Bud. Things are going great. The highway department got a big crane and cleared the debris from the bridge abutment and the road's back open again, though the water's still pretty high. We're keeping an eye on it."

"That Japanese couple will be glad to hear that. Any word on their car?"

"Well, after talking to you a bit about Tex Tanner, Hum drove over there and sure enough, it's in his lot. Tex told him he got a call to tow it."

"Was that call from a fellow named Mitt Kelso? And did you also see a red roadster in his lot?"

Cal replied, "I didn't see a roadster—are you talking about the one that woman who died had? He took that to our impound lot. But gosh, Bud, I assumed it was you or the couple who called Tanner. And why would Kelso be involved?"

"You know Kelso?" Bud asked.

"Both me and Hum have personally rescued him a time or two," Cal replied. "Which I find ironic, since he writes guide books."

"I think he and Tanner may be out there towing people's cars, then making them pay to get them back," Bud said. "It's just a theory right now, but something to think about. But I guess I need to go get the Japanese folks and take them back down there."

"I'm sure they'd appreciate that, Bud, as long as you're not too busy. But I was going to call you today. We got the coroner's report back. I'll give you a copy when you come down, but it basically says..."

Bud interrupted. "She died of selenium poisoning?"

"How'd you know that?" Cal asked.

"Cal, I think she was eating locoweed, thinking it would help cure this medical condition she had. Locoweed accumulates selenium as it grows, since it grows on toxic soils, but people actually die from this stuff in it called swainsonine, which won't show up after 48 hours, though the selenium does, making it appear that the selenium is what killed them."

"Why would she eat locoweed, since it's poisonous?"

"I think she knew that swainsonine has been found to potentially cure some diseases because it stimulates the immune system. But I think it's supposed to be isolated from the locoweed by a lab and administered under a doctor's supervision, which I doubt it was."

"So you're saying she was poisoning herself to cure herself?" Cal asked.

"Yeah, and maybe with some help," Bud replied. "Did the coroner have any ideas about what was in the mortar?"

"He said it was some kind of ground-up locoweed flower."

"That's what I figured," Bud replied. Now thinking back to Jay's question about having a positive ID, Bud asked, "Is the coroner sure it's actually Marie Lee?"

Cal was quiet for awhile, then said, "Bud, we found her ID in her pocket, the photo matched, and the car was registered to her. Why would it be someone else?"

"Just thinking out loud, Cal. She has a younger sister who looks a lot like her. Just making sure we have the right person."

Bud felt that it had to be Marie, since he'd found the mortar and pestle, which could be used to mix colors, like the article had said. And the sketch of the poisonvetch with its note, "What color!" seemed like something she would write, and there was the note from Rosalind in the jacket. But Jay's question had made him hesitate, plus, something didn't quite seem right. He thought again of the timing on the 911 call.

"I don't know how we could even ID her at this point," Cal said. "I'm pretty sure the body's been cremated. But what's going on?"

"I'm not sure, Cal, but I think things may be more complicated than they look. But is there any way I could listen to the 911 call Sandy got?"

"I think I can get her to make you a digital copy, since we record them."

"Thanks, Cal. Have her email me the file. But I should be down there in a couple of hours. I need to drop the dogs off, then go check on Howie's cats and bunny, then I'll go get that couple at the B&B and bring them down."

"Howie has a pet bunny?" Cal asked, amused.

Bud laughed. "He rescued it. It's called Little Bun."

"I always suspected he had a heart of gold," Cal replied. "But Bud, one last thing. The coroner said the body had been there about a day, which is what we originally thought. I'll see you later. Over."

Bud frowned as he got ready to go, then headed to the Melon

View B&B, fiddling with the little bird point as he drove, thinking about what Cal had told him.

Marie Lee's body had been out there for at least a day, and added to the day before they got her to the coroner, it was exactly long enough that the swainsonine wouldn't show in a lab report, though he wasn't sure at this point if that even mattered. If she'd been eating locoweed, she'd be dead anyway, but what bothered Bud was the time frame. If it had been Marie in the cafe, and Maureen had positively identified her from the picture on the back of her book, then there was no way her body could be out in the Yellow Cat. But since Marie and Rosalind looked so much alike, it was possible that Maureen had mistaken Rosalind for Marie.

Bud pulled into the circular drive of the big stately farm house, thinking of Professor Krider, who'd sold him and Wilma Jean the farm. The prof was a mystery writer and had helped Bud solve a crime or two when he'd lived there.

Bud wondered what Krider was doing, now at home down in Texas. He was probably working on another mystery, Bud mused, wishing he was here to help him solve this one, for he felt it was getting to be more than he was capable of doing.

# 33

---

"So, you guys want to go for a ride-along?" Bud asked, opening the door to the Land Cruiser and helping the Japanese couple inside.

"A ride-along?" The man asked. "I guess, if that's what you call taking us to Radium. Sure, sounds great."

"We really appreciate this," the woman added. "And we appreciate you taking such good care of us, bringing Tom here the insulin and finding us a place to stay. And that Molly, she's something special, not even charging us. We're going to send her some nice wine when we get back to California."

Bud was surprised, for he'd thought the couple didn't speak any English, as they'd been so quiet when he'd picked them up from Jasper's ambulance and taken them to the Melon View B&B. He now flashed back on Jasper asking Shorty why in heck he would need to know any Japanese.

"You're from California?" Bud asked. He'd almost said Japan, then stopped himself, realizing how provincial he'd been, thinking they were from Japan just because they looked Japanese. But hadn't Cal said they were from Japan? Maybe he and Cal both needed to get out a bit more, Bud grinned.

"We live in San Diego," the man replied. "But our daughter lives in Radium. She owns a shop there. We were going to the park, but got turned around and lost, which was bad news, since I forgot my insulin."

"I always tell him to take his insulin," the woman added with frustration.

"Well, she's right, but then we stopped and got out to climb up a hill for cell service to call our daughter. When we came back, our car was gone. We've lived in San Diego all our lives and never had anything stolen, especially something like a car. I know they call this the Wild West, but gee whiz."

"Well," Bud replied. "It's only wild when wild people come out here."

"Wild people?" asked the man.

"I think your car was illegally towed into Radium by Tex Tanner. He has a towing service. When we get down there, we're going to go pay him a visit, along with Sheriff Stocks."

Just then, the woman's phone rang. After talking a minute, she hung up, then said, "Sheriff Shumway, that was our daughter. She wants to come get us and see the B&B and meet Molly. Would you mind if we stayed and rode back with her?"

Bud replied, "No, that's fine, but be sure to hook up with the sheriff when you get down there. I think he'd like to talk to you about your car."

Bud was relieved, as he really wasn't in the mood to go to Radium anyway, although he did want to see Wilma Jean and meet little Malcolm. The town would be crawling with tourists, and he was feeling like he wanted to be alone. He'd been feeling distracted, wanting to go back out to the Yellow Cat and see if he could find out more about what had happened to Marie Lee.

He headed back to the bungalow, calling Wilma Jean as he drove.

"Hello, hon," she answered. "I was just getting ready to call you. They just released Maureen and Malcolm from the hospital, and we're all coming home, but it won't be until later, as we're all going out to lunch."

"Is everyone OK?" He asked.

"We're all fine. I stayed with Hum and Peggy Sue and it was great seeing them. They wanted us to come down for dinner, but I talked them into coming up to Green River instead. Molly and I are going to host a big dinner out at the Melon View, kind of a grand finale for the rock show. They'll come up for that. I'll probably be back there around six, hon."

Bud was relieved, glad he wasn't on his way to Radium after all. As he drove by Howie's Drive-In with its closed sign, he felt a sense of comfort, knowing things would soon get back to normal.

Stopping by his office, he checked the answering machine, then, wondering if Sandy had sent him the 911 file, booted up his computer. Sure enough, the recording was there. He clicked on the file and listened.

Sandy's voice answered: "This is 911. What is the nature of your emergency?"

Now a woman's voice came on, and she sounded panicked.

"Is this the sheriff's office?" She asked.

"It is. Do you have an emergency?"

"Yes...well...I don't know...I'm sick and need help."

"Can you please tell me your location?"

"I don't know. I'm just out in the desert. Somewhere near Green River."

"Are you alone?"

"Yes. Yes, I'm alone. Can you send someone?"

"Hang in there. I'm determining your location from your cell phone as we speak. Can you tell me what's going on?"

"I'm over by some big rocks, kind of a cliff. I've been poisoned. I'm going to die. Please help me."

"I'm sending someone out right now. Can I get your name and phone number?"

"I'm Marie Lee. I have to go. I've been poisoned. I'm from New York."

The call ended, and Bud leaned back in his chair.

The caller seemed to have a bit of a New York City accent, though

Bud wasn't entirely sure what that would sound like, though Jay seemed to also have one, and she'd identified herself as Marie Lee. But Bud was puzzled—something just didn't make sense.

Shorty had once told him that Occam's Razor, or the fact that the simplest answer was usually the correct one, was usually the best way to view things. It wasn't a good idea to make any more assumptions than necessary when trying to figure something out. And since the body was Marie's, it seemed like Occam's razor would say the caller was also Marie, but the timeline just didn't fit. Maybe he could get Jay to listen and positively identify her.

To Bud, the simplest answer was that it was Marie Lee, and she'd been poisoned by someone, maybe even herself, using locoweed, like she'd hinted at so many times in *The Last Opera Show* and had said in the call.

But was it possible that Jay had poisoned his ex-wife using locoweed, maybe giving it to her over a long period of time under the pretext that it would cure her, then persuaded her into coming out to the Yellow Cat? Was Jay hoping to hide her body where no one would find her? Had Rosalind been in on it and the one who'd made the 911 call? Did the sheet music in the fire have any significance?

Bud again thought of the morning the woman from New York had come into the Melon Rind, asking Maureen about Yellow Cat Flats. Had she been going out there to die? If so, why? But the timing was off—it had to have been Rosalind, as Marie was dead by then.

Bud took a small recorder from his desk drawer and replayed the call, recording it, then stuck the recorder in his pocket.

Now on his way home, he thought again of what Marie had said when Sandy had asked her name:

"I'm Marie Lee. I have to go. I've been poisoned. I'm from New York."

Would someone really say where they were from in a 911 call when dying? It seemed unlikely. It was almost as if she'd wanted to make a point. But why? And how in hellsbells could she have made that call when she was already at least a day deceased? Could ghosts dial cell phones and talk?

Bud pulled the bird point from his pocket, steering with one hand and fiddling with the other. He really needed to get back to the Yellow Cat, but he wanted to take care of something really important first—cleaning house before Wilma Jean got home.

## 34

Bud was tired. How in hellsbells could the house get so messy in just a couple of days? It was almost as if there was some kind of vortex around him that kicked in when his wife was gone. Surely he wasn't that messy all the time.

He'd succeeded in getting it cleaned up, though he still had laundry to do, but that could wait, for he needed a break. He'd already got the percolator pot going earlier, so he poured himself a cup of coffee and went out onto the back patio with the dogs, grabbing *The Last Opera Show* as he went.

Maybe he'd see something in it of importance, he thought, though he was about to give up, as it was starting to seem kind of garbled, the plot hard to follow. Maybe he wasn't cut out to be a mystery fan, as it was hard following all the clues, and yet he knew some people really enjoyed trying to figure things out as they went. He was more of the type to enjoy it more if he could just read the last few pages first and thereby know what clues to look for.

He opened the book to where he'd left off, though he'd mostly forgotten what was going on.

*I wheeled my BMW off the parched pavement of the highway. My tires crackled against the gravel. The pink neon sign above the doorway to the Misfitz Tavern blinked warily off and on, off and on.*

*I opened the tavern door and stepped into the darkness. The same configuration of drinkers sat near the end of the bar as last time I was there, transfixed by the TV set. They were watching a soap. Nobody had bothered to feed the jukebox. It sat there, glowing, waiting.*

*Mabel recognized me. She climbed off the stool she'd been sitting on behind the bar and asked in her low growly voice, "What'll it be?"*

*"A bottle of mineral water," I replied, and I could tell I'd made her mad.*

*I added, "I wanted to pick up a few things at the store. Know when it's going to open up again?"*

*She replied, "The man that owned it died. Ain't goin' to be open for awhile."*

*"What happened?" I tried to sound politely curious.*

*"He died a natural death. Eatin' them pistachio nuts all the time. Too much salt. Had a heart attack."*

*"A heart attack?"*

*Her eyes narrowed. "You questionin' my word? 'Cause if you are…"*

*"It'll be no trouble at all to call old Sheriff Bryce Canyon," I finished the sentence for her.*

*"Bryce Canyon? Why would I wanna call him for?"*

*"Because he always knows about everybody who died," I answered, unable to hold back the sarcasm.*

*"Maybe he knows 'cause he's sheriff," Mable said defensively. "And you mark my word. Nails is going to die from a heart attack, too. Natural causes. Too much red licorice. Anybody can see it coming."*

*"Sure seems like you folks have a lot of natural causes around here," I said.*

*Next thing I knew, Mabel was in my face. I thought for a minute she was going to deck me, but instead, she whispered, "Look, I know you're a private eye. I thought about blackmailing you, 'cause I could use the money. You know that Nails would kill you if he found out. But I have someone here who needs your help."*

*I was taken back. Who would be here that would need my help?*

*She continued. "It's Jill. She's hiding out from Nails. He wants her dead so he can have her money. She has a rare condition that nobody knows about. It's making her crazy. There's no cure. Nails was feeding her locoweed. He lied and told her he was trying to help her."*

*"I'm sorry to hear that. But if there's no cure, how could I be of any help?"*

*"Look, I know I seem like a rough character, but deep inside, I really care about Jill. She's a wonderful person, a really talented eco-artist, and she's helped me a lot. All she wants is to get some supplies and go out in the desert and paint."*

*It was one of the stranger requests I'd ever had, but how could I turn her down?*

*"Nails is on his way back. We have to go now." She pleaded. "I know where Jill is."*

*"Let's hit it," I answered.*

*The door slammed behind us just as Nails rode up on his motorcycle.*

Bud set the book down. It was starting to make even less sense than before. Who was Mable? Apparently, the bartender, but this was her first appearance, yet the P.I. knew her. Was she a character of importance? Was Marie trying to say something?

Now Bud reread a passage:

*"It's Jill. She's hiding out from Nails. He wants her dead so he can have her money. She has a rare condition that nobody knows about. It's making her crazy. There's no cure. Nails was feeding her locoweed. He lied and told her he was trying to help her."*

Nails had to be Jay, and if Jill was Marie, wasn't she implicating him in her death?

Now Bud flipped back through the book, back to a passage he'd recalled Howie reading to him earlier.

*"And if anyone's trying to get his money, it's my ex-husband. He and my father sang together at the Met, and Father trusts him. I have evidence that he wants me dead and out of the way."*

*"Why did you divorce him?" I asked.*

*"He's a very dangerous man. He likes snakes. And besides, I got tired of hearing opera all day. But now he's in a motorcycle gang."*

Did Jay like Shelby Cobras? And had he ever been in a motorcycle gang? Now Bud flipped back to where he'd been reading, for something seemed out of place.

*"Look, I know I seem like a rough character, but deep inside, I really care about Jill. She's a wonderful person, a really talented eco-artist, and she's helped me a lot. All she wants is to get some supplies and go out in the desert and paint."*

As Bud put the book down, he thought of a famous line from Shakespeare: *Methinks thou doth protest too much.* To Bud, it seemed very unlikely that a rough character like Mable would use words like *wonderful, talented,* and *eco-artist.* But then, Marie was a painter, not a writer, so maybe she didn't know about staying in character.

And to say she wanted to go out to the desert and paint? He thought back to the mortar and pestle and the ground calyx. Had she written this to create a motive for coming out here? Had she killed herself?

Maybe he was wrong, but it seemed to Bud that Marie Lee was trying a bit too hard to make herself look good and her ex-husband look bad. And then there was the passage:

*"And you mark my word. Nails is going to die from a heart attack, too. Natural causes. Too much red licorice. Anybody can see it coming."*

Now Bud flashed back again to his dream with the Widow Wilma Jean.

*Whoever stole Rosie's diary messed it all up with locoweed recipes. They also stole her snake. They want Goldie dead.*

Bud suddenly felt chilled, as if a storm were coming in. He got up and gathered the dogs, taking them inside.

Somehow, he felt that Goldie was indeed his subconscious substituting for Jay, especially since they were both large guys and had beards. He now had the feeling that Jay's life was in danger and that his death would somehow be made to look like an accident. Had Jay killed Marie, who had somehow now passed the torch to her sister, Rosalind, who was going to kill Jay for revenge?

Slipping on his jacket, Bud paused, put a load of laundry into the washing machine, then went into the bedroom and picked up his holster and Ruger.

He needed to find Jay—it was time for them to have a talk, assuming he was still alive.

# 35

---

"This lasagna's pretty good, especially for being leftovers," Bud said, leaning back in his chair in Shorty's kitchen. "But where did Jay go?"

"He's over with Molly, checking out the B&B. He's thinking about renting a room over there for awhile. He should be back any minute."

"What's wrong with here?"

"Oh, nothing, but we're getting ready to paint the exterior, and he's thinking he'll be in the way. I told him he wouldn't, but he seems like a pretty considerate guy."

"It sounds like he's planning on staying awhile. Say, Shorty, you've been around him some by now. Does he seem like the kind of guy who would kill his ex-wife? Did he say anything that could be a hint as to why he's out here?"

"He sure doesn't strike me as a murderer, Bud, but then, nobody plans a murder out loud, and they sure don't talk about it afterward, at least not if they're smart."

"Shorty," Bud said with concern. "I'm thinking that maybe Jay should lie low for awhile."

"What's going on, Bud?"

Bud explained what he'd read, as well as what Cal had said about the coroner's report. When he was done, Shorty said, "So, you're thinking Marie's sister Rosalind may be out gunning for Jay, since she may think Jay killed Marie? It does sound plausible. But he should be OK here or at Molly's, as long as nobody says anything, at least until you decide to arrest him, which I would hope you're planning to do, if he did kill her. Where is Rosalind, anyway?"

"Maybe out in the Yellow Cat, driving Jay's stolen Jeep. I think she may have tried to strangle him, then taken it. Did you notice the mark on Jay's neck?"

"Wouldn't it be more likely that Tex Tanner had towed it?"

"I don't know, but I think Tex might have second thoughts about towing a rental. It had *Cliff-Wrangler Rentals* on the side, and the company might not be too happy to see it in his lot."

"Well," Shorty replied thoughtfully. "Since her Cobra was towed, she would need some way to get around, so stealing his Jeep would make sense. But since he's not out there any more, wouldn't she be here looking for him?"

Bud replied, "That's what I'm afraid of. But something just doesn't feel right. I need to get back out there and look around some more."

"What are you expecting to find at this late stage of the game, Bud, except maybe running into Rosalind?"

"I really don't know, Shorty, but usually, when I'm working on a case, things can get confusing and convoluted, but this feels different, like maybe someone's deliberately trying to confuse things."

"Some kind of duplicity?"

"I guess you could put it that way. It feels like something that was carefully planned, but they left out a few logical steps or two. Like someone who..."

"Isn't all there?"

"Yeah, that's one way to put it, I guess. It's like looking into the mind of a person who simply doesn't think like you do."

"And just who would that person be?"

"That's what I can't quite figure out."

"Maybe someone who's a little loco. But I need to go get some paint and get started on this house. I've been putting it off too long."

"I can come over and help you later this evening," Bud said. "By the way, Wilma Jean and Molly are having a big dinner over at the Melon View, and you and Cassie are invited."

"She's back?"

"They're supposed to be on their way soon. I'll let you know when the dinner is. It's for the rock show, so it has to be soon, as that's winding down."

"Sounds good," Shorty said. "But I can hear Jay coming."

Bud could hear someone singing in a rich baritone voice:

*Ah, che bel vivere,*

*Ah, what a beautiful life,*

*La la la la!*

Jay walked in and greeted them, then put a platter of cookies on the table, saying, "This is from Molly. She says hello."

"Perfect timing," Bud replied, taking one. "Dessert after that delicious lasagna you made."

"I'll be back in a little bit," Shorty said, now standing. "Do you need anything in town, Jay? I need to get some paint."

"No, I'm fine, thanks, though that walk over to the B&B kind of wore me out. I need to get in shape," Jay said, sitting down.

Shorty nodded, then left Bud and Jay munching on cookies.

"Say, Jay," Bud said. "Would you mind listening to something and telling me what you think? I kind of hate to ask you, as it may be painful for you, but I really need your opinion."

"Painful for me?" Jay asked with surprise.

"It's a 911 call. I need to see if you can identify the voice."

He took the small recorder from his pocket and turned it on.

*Is this the sheriff's office?*

*It is. Do you have an emergency?*

Bud watched Jay closely as the call unfolded, then asked, "Do you know who the caller is?"

Jay showed no emotion as he said, "It's Marie Lee, my ex-wife, just like she said in the call."

"Are you sure?" Bud asked.

"Without a doubt," Jay replied, his face blank.

"Do you have any idea what was going on?"

"Not really," Jay said thoughtfully. "Except she sounded like she was dying."

Now Bud replayed the last of the call.

*I'm Marie Lee. I have to go. I've been poisoned. I'm from New York.*

He asked Jay, "Do you know why she would say she'd been poisoned? And where were you when she made that call?"

Jay flinched. "I have no idea why she would say she'd been poisoned nor where I was. Are you thinking I was there with her?"

Bud replied, "Were you?"

"No, or I would remember it. When did she make that call?"

"She called 911 the day I met you out at the missile base, but it can't be her. It was the same day Rosalind came into the cafe."

"It was Marie, no doubt. But Rosalind was in the cafe?"

"Jay, surely you know Rosalind's out here somewhere, though no one's seen her since then. She was inquiring about the Yellow Cat."

Jay looked puzzled, then said, "That's why you asked me if I'd seen my writer friend. Now it makes sense. I thought it was rather odd. But why would she be out here?"

"I'm trying to figure that out," Bud replied. "I thought you might know."

"No, I haven't seen Rosalind since I left New York," Jay replied.

"Do you mind if I ask what happened to your neck?" Bud asked.

Jay looked surprised, touching his neck. "I'd rather not talk about it. Let's just say it's allergies and let it go at that. But what's all this about, Bud? I feel like you're maybe thinking I did something bad."

"Did you?"

"Not that I recall."

"Look, it would help if you'd tell me why you're out here," Bud replied. "Even though you may think it's none of my business, it's actually becoming my business."

"I'm not following what you're saying," Jay dodged.

Bud sighed. "Jay, I don't want to go into why, as I think you already know, but I think your life may be in danger. It would be best if you stayed here at Shorty's until I can figure out what's going on."

"Shorty was going to take me down to get my car in Radium," Jay replied, looking worried. "Is that OK?"

Now wondering if Jay intended to return to New York, Bud asked, "Are you leaving Green River?"

Jay sighed. "I don't want to, but I don't know how I could stay."

"It's easy," Bud replied. "You just stay."

"What about money and making a living?"

Bud thought for a moment. If Jay really had anything to do with Marie's death, wouldn't he want to flee? In fact, most people would be long gone after murdering someone, especially if they had no ties to an area.

Finally, Bud said, "Jay, if you really like Green River that much and want to stay here, you could find work. It might not pay very well, but every once in awhile jobs open up. In fact, I think the mayor's looking for a gas jockey over at his station."

Jay looked thoughtful. "You mean pumping gas?"

"Well, kind of, though most people pump their own. But running the station and stuff like that."

"Well, I can't leave for awhile anyway," Jay replied. "But you know, Bud, ever since I came out here, things feel different. The things I thought were so important back home have faded away. I don't even care if I sing opera anymore, and it was my dream ever since I was a little kid."

Even though he himself couldn't imagine dreaming of singing opera, especially as a kid, Bud said, "I understand. Sometimes you achieve your goals and are ready for something different. I mean, to be made Opera Singer of the Year? That's quite an achievement, I would think."

Bud paused, then continued. "But you know, people come out here all the time and don't want to go home. Everything out here seems simple—the phone never rings, nobody expects anything of you, and your goals are easy to reach, mostly the kind that go with making it around the next bend in the river or to the top of the next ridge. And after living like we were intended to live, close to nature, not needing or wanting much, then having to leave with no idea if you'll ever return, well, I can understand how it would be hard. I could never live in the city."

"It feels like a kind of withdrawal, having to go," Jay replied. "And I haven't even been out here very long. You know, I've come to realize that merely knowing how to survive can be much easier than knowing how to live."

Now Bud stood. "That's an interesting way of putting it. I'll have to think about that one. But I need to get going, Jay. Do you mind if I ask why you said you can't leave yet? I mean, is it because you don't want to or because you can't?"

Jay shook his head. "It's both. I'm just not ready to talk about it, but I will say that it has to do with my ex-wife."

Surprised and not sure what to say, Bud nodded his head, told Jay to be careful, then walked out the door.

As he headed for the bungalow, he decided It was still early enough to go out to the Yellow Cat. Since Wilma Jean had said they wouldn't be back for awhile, he figured he had time to go pick up Lindie and make a quick trip.

He felt that something was missing, and he just needed to somehow reconcile things, though he was beginning to think it might be an impossible task.

# 36

Bud was now in his FJ instead of his sheriff's vehicle, as he felt more comfortable taking his own rig into the backcountry. Lindie sat by him, watching out the window, excited to be going.

After turning off the freeway onto the road to Yellow Cat Flats, Bud noticed the flag was up on the mailbox, so he stopped and looked inside. Instead of a letter, someone had left a note.

*If anyone knows the whereabouts of my dad Jasper Hittle, please contact me at 970-623-6881 or have him call me. I urgently need to talk to him. Willow Hittle*

Bud wrote down her name and number and put the note back. So, Jasper did have family, and Bud knew the 970 prefix was somewhere in Colorado. He doubted if he'd see the pair, but if so, he'd relay the message.

As he drove along, Bud again marveled at the lack of vegetation on the Mancos, even though he knew it wasn't entirely from a lack of water, but was also from the crumbling mudstone that swelled and contracted when it rained or dried up, making it impossible for plants to set roots. He also knew the selenium salts made growth impossible for anything but plants like locoweed.

He again thought of Marie and *The Last Opera Show* and how she'd tried to modify Rosalind's work to fit her own agenda. Now, from nowhere, just driving along, Bud suddenly wondered if perhaps he and Howie weren't themselves just characters in some mystery novel.

Laughing at the thought, he recalled the picture he'd seen of Marie and Rosalind and its caption: "Marie Lee and her younger sister Rosalind Lee in better days." He again wondered what it meant, but he guessed it was before they both knew they had porphyria.

Now dodging a rabbit that had suddenly emerged from a stand of greasewood by the road, Bud noticed a red-tailed hawk sitting on a nearby hill, watching for its dinner, and he hoped the rabbit would hide.

He thought of Howie's Little Bun and wondered if she would prefer a life out here, being free yet hiding from a host of predators that not only included birds of prey, but also coyotes and even mountain lions. He wasn't sure he himself would like it, as much as he loved the Big Empty.

He now marveled at how well he could see into the maw of the collapsed Salt Valley anticline, that geologic structure Shorty had said was responsible for the accumulation of uranium and that also held Yellow Cat Flats and the Yellow Cat Cafe. He noted that the rocks on the slopes of the anticline were much different from the Mancos, and the area bore stands of juniper trees.

He knew from Shorty's lecture that this was the Dakota formation, which was much more hospitable to plants and where small herds of mule deer lived, sometimes serving as lunch for yellow cats.

Now dropping down off the Mancos, Bud turned toward the Ringtail Mine. He was soon at the place where he'd parked before, near the rocks where Marie's body had been found.

Letting Lindie out, he grabbed his daypack, which held his camera, some water, a small bag of trail mix and an apple, and some

Barkie Buscuits. Tying his jacket to the pack, he then headed for the rocks, Lindie leading the way.

He could see the tracks from a few days back, exactly like they'd been, his own trailing alongside them from when he'd been there looking for clues. He was surprised at how well-preserved they still were, but he knew that, as long as there was no wind or weather, tracks would last a long time in the desert.

It had been a number of days since he'd been there, maybe almost a week, and he had little hope of finding anything new, but he knew if he didn't come up with something soon, the case would just get harder and harder to solve. Besides, he was beginning to feel that other matters needed his attention, like being Sheriff of Emery County, as well as Hoppie and Pierre and the melon farm.

He stood by the indentation where the body had been, then again examined the tracks going to it. If Marie was as slight as Rosalind, her tracks sure seemed deeper than he would've guessed, almost as deep as Cal and Hum's, which were nearby. He again noted how their tracks were heavier going out, as they were carrying Marie's body.

Lindie was now up in the nearby rocks, sniffing around, and Bud climbed up alongside her, recalling how they'd found Jay in a similar place, singing his heart out. Could Jay be responsible for his ex-wife's death? It just didn't seem right to Bud, but who else might it be? Would Rosalind have reason to kill her sister?

He turned, looking along the back side of the rock outcropping, noting it would be easy to climb down it. Lindie was already off it, so Bud followed her, careful to not misstep.

Once on the back of the outcropping, Bud was surprised to find more tracks! He could immediately tell they were the same as those leading to Marie's body. Had she wandered around back here before dying?

He bent and carefully examined them—they seemed shallower, but it was hard to tell if they really were or not. He found a small stick and carefully measured the depth, then climbed back to the other side and compared it to one of the tracks there.

It wasn't his imagination, the tracks on the backside of the rocks seemed much shallower than those by the body. He climbed over again and remeasured. Now sure of it, he sat on a rock, petting Lindie, wondering what was going on. Was he making something out of nothing?

Standing, he now followed the tracks, which meandered around the outcropping and eventually led back to the road, where they disappeared under the tracks of various vehicles that had gone by, one just a few moments before, judging by the dust still settling.

In fact, Bud could still see the tail end of the vehicle, and it looked just like his FJ. Looking back to where he'd parked along the road, he could see it was gone.

As he watched the vehicle disappear into the distance, Bud thought he could make out a hint of yellow as the dust settled.

It had to be Tex Tanner!

## 37

Bud figured he'd already walked a couple of miles when he sat down on a rock by the road to take a break, Lindie at his side. After giving her a Barkie Biscuit from his daypack, he ate a little trail mix, then drank from his water bottle.

Noticing Lindie watching him drink, he poured some water into a small depression in the rock, which she quickly lapped up. He needed to get one of those little collapsable dog bowls, he thought, refilling the depression several times before she seemed OK. He wondered how long a single bottle would hold the two of them—not long, he figured, even though it was cooling off with the oncoming evening.

Where were all those rockhounds when you needed them? Bud wondered, noting the sun was now beginning to set. He figured they were probably over on the road to the Cactus Rat Mine, which was the way to the Parade of Logs and other interesting sites—or more likely, they'd all gone home for the day.

Bud pulled a small flashlight from his pack. He knew he'd be able to see well enough with it, and though he had his jacket, he knew the night would still get cold. It had been a nice warm day, but he knew the lack of humidity in the desert always resulted in the temperatures dropping quickly once the sun set, and he could already feel a chill coming on.

He'd tried his cell phone several times but was unable to get service, even when he'd climbed a nearby hill. About all he knew to do at this point was to keep walking, as that would eventually get him back to the freeway, though he knew it was a good 10 miles or more. It was unlikely that anyone there would pick up a shadowy figure in the dark—but at the rate he was going, it would be morning by the time he got there anyway.

He wondered how far it was to the Yellow Cat Cafe and toyed with the idea of going there, but he knew it was probably about as far as the freeway, and he had no idea if Jasper and Leon would even be around. He again wondered what the note from Jasper's daughter had meant.

The sun was now setting, a huge golden ball slowly sliding down the distant horizon. Bud got out his camera, but with no clouds for the sun to light up, there wasn't much to photograph, and he knew he could damage his camera's sensor if he focused on the sun for too long.

He was beginning to wonder if anyone would be able to find him, even if they came looking, which wasn't very likely, as he'd neglected to leave a note for Wilma Jean, nor had he said anything to Shorty.

Wilma Jean would miss him when he didn't come home, but she would have no idea where he was. And besides, even if she or Shorty decided to come looking, finding him in the labyrinth of roads criss-crossing the Yellow Cat would be unlikely.

He searched through his pack until he found the small watertight cylinder he kept matches in, relieved. He could always build a grease-wood fire if he got cold, which he was sure he would. He knew he was close to the wash he'd walked the dogs down when he'd come out the first time, and it had been lined with plenty of the stuff.

Still sitting on the rock, Bud noted the light had changed, every-thing now taking on a rosy color. He stood and turned to see clouds behind him to the east, far over Pinion Mesa, lit up like delicate pink chiffon edged in gold. Now taking photo after photo, Bud forgot his precarious situation and instead felt that elation he often got when out in the beauty of the natural world. As the clouds slowly faded to gray, he finally put his camera back in his pack, sitting back down on the rock.

He knew he needed to get to the wash and gather some grease-wood before it got completely dark, but he instead pulled out his harmonica and began softly playing. He then began singing, Lindie now at his feet.

> Northern stars hang in the sky,
> Wind calls through the lonesome pines,
> All the world is like a dream,
> And how bright the moon can seem,
> On the Yukon Trail.

Suddenly, Lindie stood, ears perked, looking up into the rocks above them. Bud quickly grabbed her by the collar just as he could see a head appear, backlit against the final glow of the sunset, and soon the entire animal emerged.

A cat! Bud quickly pulled Lindie's leash from his pack and put it on her, then took out his camera and began taking photos, astounded by his luck. He'd wandered the Big Empty for years and never seen a single mountain lion, nor any trace of one except occasional tracks. There was a good reason they were called the ghosts of the forest—or of the desert, in this case.

As the light faded into a deep bronze color, the lion turned and looked directly at Bud, its golden fur backlit by a last ray of light. Bud knew this would be the best of all the photos, and sure enough, later, when he got back home and printed it out, Wilma Jean selected it to not only be in her annual Best of Bud calendar, along with a photo he'd taken of a bear up in the Yukon, but to also grace the wall of the Melon Rind Cafe, saying it was amazing how its whiskers looked like they were on fire.

Now the cat disappeared back into the rocks and Lindie relaxed. Bud stood and hoisted his pack onto his shoulder and headed down the road, Lindie leashed at his side, taking out his harmonica and playing as he walked, trying to calm himself a bit.

It was time to get going, collect some wood and see about starting a fire. It was going to be a long night, he figured, and he'd just as soon spend it by a nice warm fire than in the jaws of some big yellow cat.

## 38

---

"Hey, Buster, you're gonna get eaten if you wander around out here in the dark, and that harmonica ain't gonna help you!"

Bud recognized that voice—it was Jasper! He'd been ready to start a fire when he'd seen the lights of the vehicle coming toward him. He'd held out his hand, hoping whoever it was would stop, but he'd figured it would be some rockhound, late getting home.

"Well, I'll be go to wherever," Jasper said. "If it ain't Sheriff Shumway. What in hellsbells are you doing out here? Walkin' your dog?"

Bud laughed. "Any chance I could get a ride with you fellas?"

"What happened to your vehicle? Stuck?"

"No, it disappeared. I think Tex Tanner had something to do with it."

"We saw him towing a Jeep earlier today. One of those rental jobs. He sure doesn't waste time. Jump in. We can give you a ride, but only for a few miles."

Bud opened the side door of the old ambulance and climbed into the back, Lindie jumping in behind him, then asked, "Only a few miles? Is there any chance you could get me to Green River? I'll buy you dinner and fill your tank."

Jasper replied, "That would be a Jim Dandy thing to do, but we only have enough gas to go a few more miles. We'll be lucky if we get back to the cafe. No way we could even get to the freeway, yet alone Green River."

Leon added glumly, "We were hoping to find some gas over in the park, but just like you warned us, there's nobody around."

"Not even a single little goldfish cracker," Jasper said desultorily. "It's a desert over there. We're tired and hungry and are soon gonna be riding a shanksmare. And we gotta get back in less than an hour."

"Less than an hour?" Bud asked.

"It's time for the K-RAT Show," Leon replied, rolling his eyes. "Can't miss that. But I think we can maybe get back to the cafe. Could you call out and get someone to bring us some gas?"

"There's no reception out here," Bud said. "I've been trying to call out for some time."

"Looks like you'll be bunkin' with us tonight," Jasper said. "Assuming we get back. If not, we'll all be walkin' the dog."

They bounced along in the dark, Bud amazed that the ambulance didn't just fall apart as they drove along. He was equally amazed at how Jasper never hesitated when they came to the many forks in the road, knowing even in the dark which way to go.

They were soon at the Yellow Cat Cafe, to Bud's relief. He knew he could sleep in the ambulance, for they had let Jay sleep there, and it might not be real comfortable, but it would beat keeping a fire going all night and worrying about mountain lions.

"Whattya want for dinner, Sheriff? We have gourmet beef stew, teriyaki chicken, or spaghetti. Take your pick." Leon held up several freeze-dried packages.

"I don't care. Whatever you boys don't want," Bud said. He was hungry, but most freeze-dried dinners he'd had weren't all that great.

Leon replied, "I'll make you the stew. That way, you can share with the dog. What's her name, anyway?"

"Lindie," Bud replied. "Stew sounds fine."

Jasper was now fiddling with his HAM gear while Leon boiled water on a little camp stove, and Bud knew it would soon be time for their rogue radio show. He wondered if anyone ever really listened to it.

It then dawned on him that maybe Cal would be listening! Maybe he could get a message to him!

They were soon eating, and before he was even finished with his dinner, Jasper was in front of his HAM radio, an antique microphone in his hand.

*CQ, CQ, and hello out there to all you HAM radio folks, and welcome to another espeedode of K-RAT Radio, that's K-R-A-T, comin' to you from the Cactus Rat Mine and the Yeller Cat Cafe out here on the Poison Strip. We have a special treat for you tonight, but first, here's the local news.*

*The big headliner for today is that the national park has been abandon-ded. We're not sure what's goin' on, but there ain't nobody out there, so it's a good time to visit. We'd recommend coming tomorrow, since it's dark right now, and be sure to bring lots of good eats, as the ravens are hungry.*

Jasper paused, then continued in his raspy voice.

*Okie dokie, so that's that, and now we have a public PSA, that's code talk for a public service announcement. We don't get paid anything when we run these PSAs, just so you know.*

*We've been informed that there's a big need right this very moment for a special public service out at the Yeller Cat Cafe. You probably don't know this, but there's an amblance service out here, and it's the only one for many square miles. A lot of folks depend on this amblance for their food and water, and we've been informed by the amblance folks that they're plumb out of gas. So if any of you feel like doing a special service, please bring out a few gas cans—any octane will work. And here's one more PSA for you. Remember that it's important to rotate your dynomite every once in awhile to make sure it don't get unstable.*

Bud laughed. Even though what they were doing was pretty much illegal, he had to admire their audacity. Jasper continued.

*Folks, it's time for that special treat I promised you, and like that guy we had on the last show from New York City, we have another guy from another faraway place who's going to play for you, though it's not a place quite as faraway. Tonight, we have Sheriff Bud Shumway of Green River playing his harmonica. Yup, you heard me right, a real-live harmonica-playin' sheriff, right here at the Yeller Cat Cafe. Let's give him a hand, Leon.*

Leon and Jasper clapped, then Jasper asked,

*What are you gonna play for us tonight, Sheriff?*

Bud was surprised. Play on the K-RAT show? By doing so, he would be complicit in helping with a bootleg broadcast. He hesitated, then pulled his harmonica from his pocket, thinking maybe Cal was listening, and said,

*I'd like to thank you boys for having me on here, and if my good friend Cal's listening, I'd like him to know I sure would like to spend the night in my own bed and to call my wife then bring some gas out. But anyway, I'm going to play a sort of a classic, but let me say I'm still pretty new at all this, so don't get your expectations up too high.*

Bud then played a song he'd been working on for a long time, *Ghost Riders in the Sky*. He was a bit hesitant to try it, but he thought maybe he'd finally got the *yippie kiy-oh, yippie kiy-ay* part down.

He was at first a little nervous, but as he went along, he realized he had it down perfectly after all this time. A little practice goes a long way, he thought, but a lot of practice goes even farther. Leon and Jasper again started clapping. Jasper then said,

*OK, folks, after some of my famous banjo pickin', we're gonna wind things down. Be sure to listen in next week, same time, same place, for the K-RAT Show at the Yeller Cat Cafe out here in Yeller Cat Flats.*

Jasper then began playing what sounded kind of like Foggy Mountain Breakdown while Leon went outside, motioning for Bud to follow.

"I have trouble listening to that," he told Bud. "You can sleep out here in the ambulance. There's a sleeping bag in it. If you need anything, let me know. Hopefully your sheriff buddy will come out and bring us some gas. He can give you a ride home, then we'll come and collect that gas and dinner you promised us."

Bud laughed, not sure if Leon was kidding or not.

Leon continued, "I just want to let you know that we're leaving soon. A rockhound came by this afternoon with a note from the mailbox. It was from Jasper's daughter, and the rockhound had called her, as the note said to. He knew us from a day or so back, said somebody'd taken his food, so we gave him some of ours, which coincidentally was the same as his, so he was sure happy about that, not having to eat strange stuff and all."

Bud wondered if that rockhound hadn't just happened to be Paul Devlin, the one who'd reported his food stolen and given him the jacket with Rosalind's note.

"Jasper's daughter told this guy that Jasper needs to come home 'cause he's needed there on his daughter's farm. Seems like her hired guy quit and she wants me and Jasper to help do the weedin' and irrigatin'. She has a real nice old '57 Argosy trailer we can stay in, and it's a pretty uptown place, over there in Delta, Colorado. So, we're leavin' here, and it's probably a good thing, 'cause it's gonna get too hot anyway."

Bud replied, "That probably really is a good thing, Leon, though some of us will miss seeing you guys out here." He didn't add that some wouldn't, like Cal and Hum. He added, "And thanks for putting me up. See you in the morning."

Bud climbed into the ambulance and closed the door, wondering if Cal would make it out. It was getting late and would be a pretty special effort from him, if he did, assuming he'd even heard the show.

Bud was tired, and as he drifted off on the hard ambulance floor,

Lindie curled up next to him under the old sleeping bag, he suddenly remembered what Jasper had said earlier about seeing Tex Tanner:

*We saw him towing a Jeep earlier today. One of those rental jobs.*

Bud sat up. That Jeep had to have been Jay's, and Rosalind had to be out here somewhere all alone, no rig to sleep in, and who knew if she even had a coat? And was that yellow cat he'd taken the photos of anywhere nearby?

He lay back down. There was nothing he could do, but he knew he sure wasn't going to get any sleep for worrying.

Now he again thought of the dream he'd had and the line from the Widow Wilma Jean:

*Whoever stole Rosie's diary messed it all up with locoweed recipes. They also stole her snake. They want Goldie dead.*

Rosie's diary had to be the plagiarized book, and the locoweed recipes referred to eating locoweed. The snake was her Cobra, and Goldie was Jay.

He now drifted off, confident that his dream, as cryptic as it seemed, would eventually lead him to the heart of things.

## 39

Bud woke, everything around him lit with a bright blue light. It took him awhile to realize where he was, and he thought of the story of the pickup high on the cliffs, but since the light didn't change, he decided it was a vehicle outside with its lights shining directly into the ambulance.

Someone was now knocking on the door, and Lindie was wagging her tail, whacking Bud in the face with each wag. He pulled off the sleeping bag and stood, sore from sleeping on the hard floor.

"Bud, it's Hum. You in there?"

Bud opened the door, relieved, as Lindie jumped out and greeted Hum.

"I'm pretty happy to see you," Bud said. "But where's Cal? I expected him to come. Did he hear the radio show?"

Hum replied, "He did, and he called me. He's the only one on duty, as Hans is out sick, so I called your wife and she said you were missing. I brought some gas. Where's your rig?"

"Probably in Tex Tanner's lot," Bud replied solemnly.

Hum said nothing, as Bud took the can and poured the gas into the ambulance's tank.

"These guys gave me a ride, but they didn't have enough gas to get me home," he explained. "Thanks again for coming."

"No problem, but Tanner stole your vehicle right out from under you, just like that?" Hum shook his head. "It's time to put an end to this."

"He did," Bud replied. "I was over the hill, and when I came back, he was towing it away. He didn't even see me. But Hum, I think we have a bigger problem right now than Tanner."

He explained how Tanner had also towed Jay's rental Jeep, and how he suspected Rosalind was now out in the Yellow Cat, probably totally unprepared.

"How do we know she's actually out here?" Hum asked.

Jasper and Leon had now emerged from the dugout, still wearing their longjohns, and Jasper's gravelly voice replied, "Leon and I saw her yesterday evening, and she had that rental Jeep. I'd bet my last cigar she's still out here. We warned Sheriff Shumway here that Tanner was up to no good, and that guy Kelso is in on it."

Hum looked questioningly at Bud, who nodded his head in agreement.

Now Hum said, "Bud, we can't just go blindly out looking for her without some idea where she might be, especially in the dark. We're talking a few hundred square miles of wilderness."

"Agreed," Bud replied. "But I know somebody who would know a good place to start looking, if you could get ahold of him."

"Tanner?" Hum asked.

"Exactly," Bud replied. "Radio Cal and have him go to Tanner's house and get him up. Find out where he hooked up that Jeep."

"Good idea," Hum replied, going to his pickup. He was soon back, saying, "Cal's on it. He'll radio me back when he finds out. And by the way, that couple from San Diego came in today and are going to press charges against Tanner for stealing their car. And they're also suing Kelso for misinformation and have a good chance of winning, since the guy's an attorney and knows the ropes."

"You can put my name on the list," Bud said. "And probably Jay

Landowska's, too. He's the one with the rental Jeep. But Hum, it's cold out here. Can we go sit in your pickup?"

"Good idea," Hum replied, then, looking at Leon and Jasper, said, "You boys might as well go on back to bed. There's nothing you can do here, but you owe me for a can of gas. And just for the record, I have a dozen campers from over in the park who are willing to press charges against you two for theft of their gear and gas, including some good eye witnesses. But I'll deal with you after we sort all this out."

Jasper, looking irritated, turned and went into the dugout, leaving Leon behind, who now stood wringing his hands, pleading, "Look, Sheriff Stocks, we didn't mean any harm by it, we were just tryin' to get by. You know all them campers have money, they're tourists. None of what we took was worth much. Right, Sheriff Shumway? And we got some of it from entering contests."

Bud shrugged his shoulders, saying, "Didn't I hear you were planning on leaving the country, going on over to Colorado? Any idea when? We just put five gallons of gas in your rig, so you should be able to go anytime."

Now Leon looked relieved. "Well, if you'd be kind enough to give us a little cash so we can get all the way over there, I can guarantee we'd be gone by tomorrow, though we'll have to close down the cafe."

Hum didn't look pleased. "You should have enough to get you out of the county. After that, you're on your own. But if I see you back around here, I'll arrest you before you can say sic 'em. You won't have to worry about gas and groceries in jail."

Leon ducked into the dugout as Bud grinned, then asked, "Do you really have eye witnesses ready to testify against them?"

"No," Hum replied. "The park's not even in my jurisdiction, that's the Feds, though we sometimes help them out. But if they go to Colorado, it'll have the same effect as putting them in jail, but be a lot cheaper."

Bud and Hum got into Hum's truck, and he turned on the engine, letting the heater warm things up. Lindie sat in the middle, her head on Bud's lap, and he thought again about training her to be a SAR dog. She sure seemed to have the temperament for it, but he wasn't so sure *he* did.

Now Bud asked, "Hum, did you tell Wilma Jean you were coming out here? Is there any way you could let her know I'm OK?"

"Sure, Bud, I can radio the state troopers and have them get a message to her, but they'll probably wake her up."

"Knowing my wife, she's probably up anyway, worrying. Did you get to see Howie's baby? Wilma Jean said she and Howie stayed at your place. Is everything OK?"

"I didn't actually see the baby," Hum replied. "But Howie's walking on Cloud Nine."

Hum now got on the radio and contacted the State Patrol office in Green River, requesting that the officer on patrol in that area take a message to Wilma Jean. He paused, asking Bud, "What exactly do you want me to tell her?"

"Ask her to make me an apple pie."

Hum grinned as he relayed the message. Just as he put the mic back in its holder, a call from Cal came in.

"Hum, I got Tanner out of bed, and he was boilin' mad. He said he picked up the Jeep out by Lost Spring Canyon. It was parked on the cliffs above the spring. He said he got a call to come get it, but there was nobody out there, so he assumed they got a ride out. Over."

"Well, that's interesting," Hum replied. "Especially since last time I was out there, there wasn't any cell service. OK, Cal, thanks for doing that. Bud and I are going to drive on over there and see what we can find. Over."

"You're not gonna see much in the dark. Over." Cal answered.

"Maybe not, but we have to give it a shot. You hold down the fort. Over."

"I wish I did work at a fort," Cal replied. "Cause then I could shut the gate and lock everybody out. My tally so far tonight is three drunks, two who were fighting outside Woody's Tavern, one missing bicycle, and two car lockouts. I'm going to need a day or two to recover from all this. But you boys be safe out there. Watch out for them yellow cats. Over."

Cal's voice now faded into the distance, and Bud took out his camera, showing Hum the photos he'd taken earlier of the mountain lion.

Hum whistled, then said, "Well, fortunately Lost Spring Canyon's nowhere near where you were. How in hellsbells do you think she ended up way over there? That drains into Salt Creek, which is a big drainage. Lost Spring was just recently annexed into the park, so we'll be in their territory."

Bud replied, "I have no idea why she's over there, but I think we should get going. But if we haven't found her by morning, maybe we can get the park to help."

Now Bud pointed to the thermometer readout on the truck's display and added, "It's currently 48 degrees and is getting colder by the minute. I don't think she's prepared for the cold, Hum, and I think one dead body out here is enough for awhile."

Hum nodded his head in agreement, then turned his truck around and headed down the bumpy dusty road, Bud and Lindie happy for the warmth, as well as the comfort of being with someone who was competent and could get 'er done.

## 40

Bud and Hum hadn't gone more than a half-mile when they could see a pair of headlights coming toward them. When the lights drew near, Hum slowed, and an old pickup stopped.

"You haven't seen a lost sheriff anywhere have you?" Shorty asked good-naturedly. "We're missing one up in Green River."

Bud grinned. "Seems like the Yellow Cat's the place to be," he joked. "But how did you guys know to come out here?"

"Wilma Jean called me some time ago and said you were missing, so I called Cal, thinking he might know your whereabouts. He said he'd heard you play on the K-RAT show. Why didn't you let us know you were going live with your harmonica?"

Bud laughed, then said, "Thanks for coming. I'm glad you came, too, Jay. Hum, this is Jay Landowska, the opera singer."

Both vehicles were soon headed down the road, Hum leading. Just like Jasper had done, each time they came to an intersection, Hum seemed to know which way to go. Finally, Bud said, "You're pretty familiar with this country, eh?"

Hum replied, "Well, somewhat, but having an on-board GPS helps a lot." He pointed to the readout on his dash.

Bud said, "Hum, I know it's unusual to do a search after dark, but this gal we're looking for has a rare genetic condition called porphyria. They call it the vampire disease because it causes extreme sensitivity of the skin to light. People with it do everything in the dark and hide out during the day. I'm worried that, instead of staying put in the dark like most people would, she's out wandering around and is going to get hurt. It's urgent that we find her."

"I'm just wondering how much of a head start she has on us, Bud. If Tanner towed her vehicle earlier today, she could be miles away. Us just wandering down the canyon looking for her in the dark could be a complete waste of time. We need to get Wilma Jean out here tomorrow to fly us around in her plane."

"Understood," Bud replied. "But maybe Lindie can help us track her."

"Does she know how?"

"Probably not," Bud replied. "But we have to try."

"Agreed. Remember that preacher's wife lost out here some time ago? Everyone was about to give up on her, but we did find her, and none too soon. It snowed two feet out here the day after we found her."

They drove on, Hum now slowing as the road got rougher and rougher.

"There's not a lot of traffic out here," Hum said. "This road dead ends just above the spring at a kind of parking area. The only people I've ever seen out here are rockhounds and an occasional pipeline inspector, though they mostly do that from the air now."

Finally at the end of the road, Hum stopped, and he and Bud got out as Shorty and Jay pulled up behind them.

Hum opened the cover of his pickup bed and took out a large searchlight, as well as several smaller flashlights, handing them each one.

"We need to stick together so we don't have two searches going on. If you need to stop, let the guy in front of you know, and stay in sight of each other. The slowest guy sets the pace."

"That would be me," Jay said. "Maybe I should stay here in the truck. I'm not in that great of shape."

Bud said, "Jay, I think you should come. If you get too tired, I'll walk back out with you while Shorty and Hum continue the search. You might come in handy if we find her, since she knows you, and I suspect she's a bit disoriented by now."

"I agree," Hum said, starting down an old road that appeared to drop into the canyon, his searchlight making everything glow.

They were soon by an old corral near a stock tank fed by an old rusted pipe coming from a small crevasse in the sandstone wall. This must be Lost Spring, Bud mused, though it didn't seem all that lost or hidden. Some stockman had years ago improved it for his stock.

Bud shone his light on the brackish water, chunks of moss floating on the surface, thinking one would have to be pretty thirsty to want to drink it.

Now Lindie was wagging her tail, nose to the ground.

"Tracks!" Bud said. "And they're small, like a woman's. Good job, Lindie!"

They continued on down into the canyon, and were soon on the bottom, where they began slogging through sand, the going slow. There were times they had to push their way through tangles of desert holly and stands of willows, now walking along a small stream. Bud was amazed at how different it was from up on top, a world of water and greenery instead of toxic lifeless soils.

Now Hum stopped, shining his light up the side of the canyon wall to a scene from another era. Painted on the sandstone were tall human-sized figures that towered above them, shaped like elongated triangles, wearing robes with intricate designs of birds and points and even stars.

"Barrier Canyon," Bud said, searching through his pockets for the tiny bird point he'd found by the Ringtail Mine.

"What's Barrier Canyon?" Jay asked.

Bud explained, "It's a style of rock art, petroglyphs, made by what're called the Archaic people of some 5,000 or more years back.

The only place it's found is in southeastern Utah. The Great Gallery over in Canyonlands is the type style."

"It's kind of spooky out here," Jay replied.

"Hang on guys, I have something I need to do," Bud said. He walked over beneath the tall figures and carefully placed the tiny bird point in the rocks, then rejoined the group.

They continued on until Hum stopped them, pointing his light upwards. An arch!

"I don't know if this one has a name or not," Hum said.

"How did you know it was there?" Jay asked.

"I've been down here before," Hum replied. "On another search similar to this."

The night seemed as if it would never end as they bushwhacked their way down the drainage. Finally, the canyon seemed to widen, the vegetation getting sparser.

Now, from nowhere, Jay, who Bud knew must be getting tired, began singing.

> Poor wandering one,
> Though thou hast surely strayed,
> Take heart of grace, thy steps retrace,
> Poor wandering one.

They stopped, Shorty saying, "That seems appropriate, Jay. It's from the Pirates of Penzance, isn't it?"

Jay replied, "Yes, Mable sings it to Frederick, who's been apprenticed to the pirates until he's 21. The problem is, he was born on February 29th in a leap year, so he's not going to be 21 for a very long time."

"You have an exceptional voice," Hum said.

"Thanks. I'm no Pavarotti, but I get by."

As they stood in the dark for a moment, catching their breath, Lindie began whining. Bud shone his light on her, noting she was pawing at something on the ground.

Bud recalled the SAR dog commands Jody had sent him and said, "Find it, Lindie, find it!"

Lindie now pulled on her leash in the direction of the canyon wall, and as Bud followed he saw tracks meandering through the sand, the same tracks they'd seen earlier and that looked exactly like those he'd found over by the Ringtail Mine!

## 41

---

They were soon over by the wall, Hum shining his big light all around. The tracks had stopped there, but they soon saw a narrow ledge going up, just wide enough for someone to climb, though treacherous.

Shining the light farther up, Hum stopped at a place where a small single-leaf ash had managed to root into a small crack between the ledge and the wall.

"There!" Bud said. "Someone's behind that tree!"

The figure held their arm up, trying to shield their eyes from the light, and Bud said, "Hum, take the light off. It could cause them to lose their bearings and fall."

Hum switched off the light, and the canyon was suddenly filled with a darkness comprehensible only to those who spent their lives there, the coyotes and rabbits and deer and badgers and ringtail cats and even the giant desert centipede, the true citizens of the canyons.

Now the figure above began talking, and there was no doubt it was a woman.

"Who's shining that light? Is that you, Father? I changed the book, just like you asked me."

Now Jay started toward the woman, but Bud held his arm out,

stopping him, whispering, "Don't let Marie know you're here. It'll mess everything up."

Jay touched Bud's arm as if to say he understood.

Hum whispered, "Marie? I thought we were looking for Rosalind. Marie's the dead one, Bud."

"No, this is Marie, Hum. She poisoned Rosalind. I wasn't completely sure until just now. I'll explain later."

Now Bud yelled up to the woman, "I'm Private Eye Weatherby, and I'm looking for Jill Thaddeus. Is that you, Jill?"

"Weatherby?"

"You know, the detective you hired to figure out what was going on with your father. He was turning into a werewolf, remember? He invited me to go see his bats."

Hum whispered to Shorty, "What in hellsbells is he talking about?"

Shorty replied, "I have no idea."

Now Jay whispered, "She's totally lost it and thinks she's a character in her own book. Bud's playing along."

Now Marie asked, "Is that really you, Weatherby?"

"It's me, Jill. You need to come down, sweetheart, you and I have a date, remember? We're going out to dinner at that fancy restaurant, what was its name?"

"The Hotel Irvine?"

"Yes, that's the one. Come on down. What are you doing out here, anyway? You're going to catch a cold."

"But where's Nails? I'm hiding from him. He wants to kill me."

"Don't worry about him, sweetheart. I've taken care of Nails—for good. Let's go get some eats. Come on down, but be careful."

Bud now whispered to Shorty and Jay to stay back out of sight.

Marie began carefully inching her way down the cliff. It seemed like it took forever, but she was finally down, Bud at her side, putting his arm around her shoulders, noting that she was shivering.

"You're really a handsome guy," she said weakly. "I think this must be the first time we've actually met, outside of the book, I mean."

Bud, now carefully steering her by her elbow, soon reached Hum, saying, "Now, don't worry sweetheart, this is my chauffeur, and we're all going to hike back out together, and then he's going to take us to the Hotel Irvine."

After Bud wrapped his coat around her, they began the slow and long walk back, Hum leading, Jay and Shorty staying back out of sight.

Marie walked along quietly, as if she were totally spent, and Bud began to wonder if she would make it out. After what seemed like forever, they were back at the spring, then eventually on top, where Hum opened the back door of his club cab and Marie quietly tumbled in.

"Let's try out these special silver bracelets I bought just for you and see if they fit, sweetheart," Bud said as Hum slipped handcuffs on her.

Jay and Shorty soon arrived, and Jay got into the back of Hum's truck beside Marie. A barrier separated the back from the front, and Hum asked Jay, "You feel comfortable riding back there?"

Jay replied, "She's cuffed, so what can she do? Besides, she wasn't able to kill me earlier, even without the cuffs." He touched the red place on his neck.

Now Marie looked at Jay, confused, and said, "Jay? What are you doing here?"

"I'm here for you, Marie, like I always said I would be."

Marie looked disoriented, then put her head on Jay's shoulder and began sobbing, saying, "I poisoned my own sister, didn't I? How could I do something like that?"

"You're not well," Jay replied, looking like he himself might cry. He put his arm around her and held her close, then, ever so softly, said:

> Come away, O human child!
> To the waters and the wild
> With a faery, hand in hand.
> For the world's more full of weeping than you can
>     understand.

Hum closed the back door, got in, and they drove away.

———

"That was from a poem by W.B. Yeats," Shorty said as he and Bud leaned against Shorty's pickup, watching Hum's taillights recede into the blackness of the empty desert. "Where will they take her?"

Bud replied, "Radium has a very good hospital with a secure ward for people like Marie. The staff's very good, and they'll put her under observation, then decide what to do. But I have a feeling she's not ever getting back out. And with her condition, she may not live that much longer, anyway."

"And you played the detective in her book? Well done, my friend."

Bud said quietly, "Thanks, Shorty, but I'm only now realizing that *The Last Opera Show* wasn't a mystery after all, but a tragedy that would've made even Shakespeare proud."

Shorty put his hand on Bud's shoulder, and they stood there for awhile, looking up at a sky filled with more stars than they could ever imagine, then got into Shorty's pickup and headed back to Green River, where Wilma Jean hugged him, then read him the riot act for leaving his clothes in the washing machine.

## 42

Bud sat with Jay at the table in Shorty's kitchen, Lindie, Hoppie, and Pierre at his feet, Jay eating red licorice and helping Bud count the money in a jar from the rockhound dinner the previous night. The jar had been next to a sign that Wilma Jean had carefully hand-lettered to read: *Welcome Home Malcolm McPherson! Please donate to Malcolm's college fund.*

It had been kind of a joke, simply a way to gather a little money to help Maureen and Howie buy a new crib and changing table, but Bud and Jay had just reached several hundred dollars and were still counting.

Bud had no idea that rockhounds could be so generous, as he'd always thought they weren't a particularly well-heeled bunch, especially judging by their clothes and vehicles, but the dinner had been a big success, especially the "Retro Meatloaf" Wilma Jean had served.

Howie and Maureen and little Malcolm had made a brief appearance before the dinner started, just to say hello, as they wanted to get Malcolm home to bed. Bud marveled at how they'd managed to look so tired and yet so radiant at the same time.

Later, once the dinner was in full swing, Eldon and Frosty had shown up with Mrs. Jensen, but instead of hanging onto Frosty's every word, she'd seemed more interested in Eldon, much to Frosty's relief. Bud found out later that she and Frosty were having a tiff after she'd realized that what she'd offered to finance was alcoholic watermelon spritzer.

For some reason, Bud now thought of Jasper and Leon, wondering if they'd flown the coop for Colorado, though he suspected that, given the looks on their faces when Hum had read them the riot act, they were long gone. He knew they were smart enough to get going when the going was good.

Now Jay leaned back, the counting done, and said, "Wow, $522.76! Not bad! And when I get some money, Bud, I'm going to donate a whole lot more than that!"

"That's really nice of you, Jay," Bud replied. "But are you going to have to go down to Radium and testify against Tex Tanner?"

"Sheriff Stocks told me the DA's got a plea agreement that they think Tanner's attorney will go for and there won't be a trial. It includes some jail time. Didn't they tell you that? You're a witness, too, since he stole your FJ. You got it back, didn't you?"

"I did. Cal brought it up for me since I've been busy helping Wilma Jean at the cafe, as Maureen's off. And since Howie's busy with his drive-in and the baby, I'm covering for him at the office, not that there's much to cover. Have you heard anything about Kelso?"

"I should be back in time to testify for that one. You're in on the lawsuit against him for helping Tanner, aren't you?"

"I am, but I'm kind of out of the loop. I bet he'll want to to settle out of court. But are you coming back from New York?"

"I am," Jay replied. "But I've been meaning to ask you, how did you know it was Marie out there instead of Rosalind? I mean, I knew it was Marie, but apparently nobody else did."

Bud replied, "It took me awhile, eh? But it was a bunch of things. I started to feel like the whole thing was contrived—the sketch of the locoweed plant, the mortar and pestle put in an obvious place to make sure people knew Marie had been there looking for pigment, the jacket hanging on a bush right by the road with its dramatic note, the comments here and there in the book about how Nails, who I figured out was supposed to be you, was out to get Jill, who was Marie, and even the fact that she took Rosalind's book and inserted all this incriminatory stuff in it—it all started to add up. Then, when she was up on the cliff and started talking to her father as if she was Jill in the book, telling him she'd changed everything like he'd told her..."

"I had no idea she'd killed Rosalind, Bud. I didn't even know Rosalind was out there."

"I know that, Jay. I always assumed you were innocent, though there were a few times I had my doubts. She tried too hard to make it look like you did it. You do realize part of her plan was to kill you out there where no one would find you, though she didn't realize there were rockhounds everywhere. She wanted everyone to think you'd killed *her*, then mysteriously disappeared. But surely you knew something was up when I told you we'd found Marie's body?"

"I just figured it was somebody else. I knew Marie was still alive, and I thought Rosalind was still back in New York, so I thought you were mistaken."

"But how about the fact that Marie was driving Rosalind's car?"

"I did ask her about that, and she said Rosalind had loaned it to her, as hers had broken down. She told me she was out here looking for locoweed to try to cure their porphyria."

"But she tried to kill you."

"She did, Bud, but by then, her mind was starting to go. It was actually starting to go when she divorced me. I knew that and was terribly worried about her. That's why I followed her out here."

"Why didn't you share that with me? We could've been on the same team and thereby much more effective."

"I really don't know. I guess deep inside I was hoping she'd just come out of it and we'd go home. And like I said, I had no idea Rosalind was dead."

"Shorty says you're inheriting everything Rosalind had."

"The estate attorney back in New York told me that Rosalind had made me her sole beneficiary. She and I have always been friends, and I guess she had a lot of money, Bud, plus her car's worth a fortune. Their dad left them both a nice sum including buying them both Cobras, but Marie spent her inheritance like a drunk sailor, no offense to drunk sailors—trips to Europe, that kind of thing. I tried to get her to save it, but I think the porphyria was starting to affect her even then. She divorced me, saying I was after her money. That really broke my heart, Bud. I loved her dearly."

"And you had no idea she was planning on killing Rosalind, who also had porphyria, by feeding her locoweed under the pretense the swainsonine would cure her?"

"I don't even know what swainsonine is, Bud," Jay said glumly. "But I still don't understand why she would want to kill her. They'd been good friends, and they both started coming down with the porphyria at around the same time and had seemed to kind of band together trying to deal with it."

"Maybe she didn't start out trying to kill her and really thought the locoweed would help, then realized Rosalind was dying and she could benefit from that. In fact, if Marie hadn't put all that stuff in the book, we might be persuaded to think she'd concocted her plot after realizing Rosalind was dying, and she would be less culpable. I doubt if she even knew the swainsonine was supposed to be isolated by a lab and administered by a doctor. But since she inserted it all in a book that she somehow got published, we have a very clear intent."

"I don't understand what she was trying to do, Bud," Jay said.

"She was going to impersonate Rosalind and get her money, Jay. She talked Rosalind into coming out here, which Rosalind probably would never have done if she'd been in her right mind. Marie had been studying locoweed and discovered a very toxic type that grew only in the Yellow Cat. After doing a little research, she discovered how remote the area was and decided it would be the perfect place to kill Rosalind, then kill you, as you would be the only one who could figure out what she'd done."

"That really hurts," Jay said.

"Don't forget, she wasn't her normal self, Jay." Bud replied. "Locoweed can cause aggression. She and Rosalind came out the day before you and I met, and Marie got her to go out by the Ringtail

Mine, where she persuaded her to eat a bunch of that very poisonous strain of locoweed. I doubt if Rosalind lasted long. Marie then set up the mortar and pestle, hoping someone would find them and think she'd been out there to gather pigment, creating a reason for her to be there, especially since she had a reputation for searching out rare colors for her paintings. She wanted everyone to think she, Marie, had been killed, when it was really Rosalind. She then built a small fire, burning sheet music from Gilbert and Sullivan, trying to implicate you as being at the scene, though I don't think she thought that one through very well, as it didn't make a lot of sense."

"I'm surprised she was able to think any of it through, Bud. She was pretty far gone."

"One thing she didn't think through was hanging her red jacket on a bush by the road where someone would find it, trying to make it look like it was Rosalind's—it was kind of a red herring, so to speak. The photo I saw on the Internet said that Rosalind was wearing black until they found a cure—I assumed for porphyria. She wouldn't have been wearing a red jacket."

Bud paused as Jay nodded in agreement, then continued. "I'd found a notebook earlier where Marie had been practicing Rosalind's signature, probably prior to writing the note she put in the jacket pocket and maybe in preparation to signing Rosalind's checks and whatnot. She even switched her ID and all with Rosalind's. But anyway, after Rosalind died from the locoweed, Marie carried her body up by the rocks. She then slipped out behind the rocks and drove away in Rosalind's car, leaving her own car there, making it look like she, Marie, had come out there and died all alone. That was the car Tex Tanner towed to Hum's impound lot, the one with the IPAINT plates."

Bud paused to catch his breath, then said, "She then came into Green River to get supplies and a jack, as she must've gotten stuck at some point, maybe getting out with the help of some rockhounds. She was now posing as Rosalind, driving the Cobra with the IWRITE plates, but she didn't want to be noticed, as she was supposed to be in New York. But she was looking for you. That's why, when Maureen told her to ask me if I'd seen anyone wanting to go out to the Yellow Cat, she took off. It's kind of ironic that Maureen knew it was Marie, the author of *The Last Opera Show*."

Bud paused, thinking, then added, "Marie then went back out to the Ringtail Mine to see if anyone had discovered Rosalind's body. They hadn't, so she made that 911 call, wanting everyone to believe she was the one dying. Hum and Cal went out and retrieved the body, but Marie forgot about the coroner and how he would know the body had been there since the previous day. She messed up the timeline by not calling the same day she killed Rosalind. She then started looking for you—she must've known you were going out there, right?"

"Yes, I'd been looking for her. Once I figured out where she'd gone from all the maps and research she left at her apartment, I followed her out there."

"And that's when I met you at the missile base. You had keys to her apartment?"

Jay hesitated, then said, "I did, but she didn't know it. She left a set on her counter and I took them when she wasn't looking. Like I said, she was declining rapidly and I was worried about her. But yes, she knew I was out in the desert because I'd caught up to her in the rental Jeep."

"Jay, did it occur to you that she wanted you to be able to get into her apartment and figure out where she'd gone, because she wanted you to follow her so she could kill you? After that, she could assume Rosalind's identity, then go back to New York and liquidate Rosalind's assets and conveniently leave town. They looked enough alike that I think she could've pulled it off."

Jay looked shocked. "You really think that's what was going on? She did try to strangle *me*."

"I'm really sorry that happened, Jay. I know you love her."

"*Loved* her, Bud."

Bud was silent. Finally, Jay said, "Hum called me last night after he and his wife got back to Radium from the dinner. Marie passed away in the hospital. Congestive heart failure. She'd been eating the locoweed, too, you know, since she also had porphyria."

"I'm sorry to hear that, Jay. Is there anything I can do?"

"No, but thank you. I don't think I've even really processed it yet. I'm going back to New York in a few days to take care of everything, then I'm coming back, Bud. I need to be here, not there."

"What about Marie's Cobra?"

"I think it will probably become the property of the State of New York, unless Marie somehow left a will, which I don't think she did. There's a small chance it will be mine, but with Rosalind being so generous, I'll have plenty of money. Besides, Shorty's asked me to take over his place here. I guess he talked to your wife about it and she liked the idea and offered Molly's help to get it started. I'm going to turn it into a B&B."

Bud leaned back in his chair. "A B&B? That's perfect, Jay. You'd be the perfect guy for that—and you could give garden concerts."

Jay smiled. "I think I'm pretty much done with opera, Bud. Might as well go out while at the top of my game, and I think singing while looking for Marie was my last opera show. But Cassie wants me to help with the high-school drama club, which sounds like fun, and I did enjoy singing on the K-RAT Show, so who knows? But I'm going to call this place *The Wandering One B&B* in Marie's honor."

Bud was quiet, leaning down to pet Lindie.

Finally, Jay added, "But I haven't given it all up completely—I want to write musicals. In fact, I'm working on one that's set out in Yellow Cat Flats. Want to hear some of the lyrics?"

Bud grinned, nodding yes.

> New York City is a lonesome place,
> You don't know nobody and they're all in your face.
> Them boys up on Wall Street, they dress so fine,
> They think life ain't worth livin' if you don't have a
>     dime.
> But here in the desert, with the coyotes and stars,
> You don't need no money, at least not so far.
> You can see a long way on a real clear day,
> And life's real special, cause you've found your way.

La-la-la-la-la-la-la.

Bud laughed. "That's great, Jay. I know it'll be a big hit, if you can figure out who the audience would be."

Jay grinned, saying, "It's no Yeats, but it does describe how I feel." He paused, listening, and added, "And guess what? My first B&B client is here! It sounds like my good friend Ricky just drove up—he's from Chicago. He's got a Mark Twain show and is on tour, but will stay a few days. We're going to help Shorty paint his house and maybe even go out to the Yellow Cat and try our hand at rock-hounding."

Bud looked out the window, where a red lifted 4-by-4 Yugo had just pulled into the drive with plates that read *I-ACT*. Bud grinned and said, "Well, just don't get stuck."

Now fiddling with the harmonica in his pocket, Bud stood, adding, "I need to get back out there, too, before the wildflowers are all faded. Maybe we'll run into each other. And Jay, you were right. I'm going to train Lindie to be a search-and-rescue dog. I think she has what it takes, and I hope I do, too."

Jay smiled, and they walked out the door and on to better things.

———

If you enjoyed this book, check out the next in the series, The Swiftcurrent Cafe.

# ABOUT THE AUTHOR

Chinle Miller writes from southeastern Utah and western Colorado, where she spends most of her time wandering with her dogs. She has an A.S. in Geology, a B.A. in Anthropology and an M.A. in Linguistics.

If you enjoyed this book, you'll also enjoy the other books in the Bud Shumway mystery series:

*The Ghost Rock Cafe*
*The Slickrock Cafe*
*The Paradox Cafe*
*The No Delay Cafe*
*The Silver Spur Cafe*
*The Ice House Cafe*
*The Rattlesnake Cafe*
*The Beartooth Cafe*
*The Melon Rind Cafe*
*The Cessna Cafe*
*The Klondike Cafe*
*The Yellow Cat Cafe*
*The Swiftcurrent Cafe*
*The Sunnyside Cafe*
*The Temple Mountain Cafe*

And don't miss *Desert Rats: Adventures in the American Outback*, *Uranium Daughter*, *Wandering off the Map*, and *The Impossibility of Loneliness*, also by Chinle Miller.

And if you enjoy Bigfoot stories, you'll love *Rusty Wilson's Bigfoot Campfire Stories* and his many other Bigfoot books, as well as his popular *Chasing After Bigfoot: My Search for North America's Most Elusive Creature*.

Other offerings from Yellow Cat Publishing include an RV series by RV expert Sunny Skye, which includes *Living the Simple RV Life*, *The Truth about the RV Life*, and *RVing with Pets*, as well as *Tales of a Campground Host*. And don't forget to check out the books by Sunny's friend, Bob Davidson: *On the Road with Joe* and *Any Road, USA*. And finally, you'll love Roger Dean Miller's comedy thriller, *Bombing Hoffman*.

www.ingramcontent.com/pod-product-compliance
Lightning Source LLC
Chambersburg PA
CBHW021221260626
47172CB00002B/532